The Awful Truth . . .

Jim telephoned when she was at her lowest. Janey couldn't sound anything but what she felt: beat.

"Just what did you have for dinner?" he demanded. "Don't say food. Tell me."

Because it was impossible to lie when she looked into his stern blue eyes—and on the phone she always closed her eyes and imagined them—she told the truth.

"Are you trying to kill yourself?" he roared. "Do you know what happens to girls who don't eat properly?"

"Umhum," she said. "They hold their jobs..."

PUT PLEASURE IN YOUR READING
Larger type makes the difference
This EASY EYE Edition is set in large, clear type—at least 30 percent larger than usual. It is printed on scientifically tinted non-glare paper for better contrast and less eyestrain.

A Measure Of Love
Jeanne Bowman

EASY EYE

VALENTINE BOOKS
NEW YORK

EASY EYE A VALENTINE BOOK

A MEASURE OF LOVE

Valentine Books are published by
PRESTIGE BOOKS, INC., 18 EAST 41ST STREET
NEW YORK, N.Y. 10017

Chapter One

It was raining. And it wasn't raining daffodils. Long lines of moisture, pointed at the ends, streaked down from a dark March sky to stab defenseless pedestrians.

Women scurrying past the pale gold foyer of a dress salon (so sacrosanct its windows carried only the world *Elaine*) glanced at the girl just outside the door. If they were old they sniffed and swam on. If they were young they hesitated, then looked wistful and wondering.

They had recognized the girl. Who wouldn't? She was Elaine's favorite model, who appeared regularly on television and in newspaper ads. They also noticed the moisture in the girl's eyes. Imagine having a plush job like hers and crying!

Men passed, huddled in topcoats. They looked once, then looked again and stopped huddling. No girl as lovely as that must see them stooped over. Let the rain run down their collars.

One older man in the delivery livery of Elaine brushed past, then stopped. "Come on, Janey. I have a drop-off in your neighborhood."

"Thanks, Ted." Janey rushed out to squish beside him. "I just couldn't call a cab."

"Yeah, I know. We heard her dressing you down. Wouldn't do for her to see you cry."

"That wasn't why. I knew if I opened my mouth even to call a cab, I'd blow up."

"What did you do to bring on her wrath?"

Janey waited until they were in the cab of the truck, then blurted, "Gained four pounds."

"That's not much."

"Ted, think of it as four pounds of butter in all of the wrong places. The Medina girl came in for her trousseau, and I had to model it because we are, or rather were, the same size. The wedding gown had a basque waist. When they zipped me in it looked awful."

"Why didn't they try it on the one it was made for?"

Janey gave him a pitying look. "Clothes always look better on models," she explained.

By some alchemy known only to truck drivers, Ted had caught each green light, swung into a hill boulevard and now came to a stop before an imposing apartment house.

"Sure no place for the unemployed to live," he said heartily. And Janey, stricken afresh, scurried under the nose of a supercilious doorman who stalked out to tell delivery truck drivers where to go.

Unemployed. She shuddered in the perfumed

warmth of the foyer, of the elevator, of the very top floor. Where did the unemployed live? And how could she explain to anyone Elaine insisted upon a "good address and good morals" for all her front employees? Janey was the frontest of the front.

"Squirrel cage," she announced solemnly, once she had gained the long living room. "Round and round and you never catch up."

Three pair of eyes looked out from the dinette embrasure. "You're late again," remarked the one with the oldest eyes.

"I've been fired again," Janey retorted.

"Almost?" asked the youngest.

"How many pounds this time?" came the weary question of the middle one.

"Four."

She walked close to the table and didn't quite groan. Martha had made that casserole again: raw brown rice, ground beef, button mushrooms, and on top wads of cashew nuts. And she was nearly starving to death.

"Martha forgot to add the chicken broth; you can have a cup of that."

"Skimmed," added Martha. "That girl knows one photographs twice as large as life. We protect her figure with a balanced diet. And what does she do when we're not watching?"

Ina, the youngest, sprang to her defense. "A girl can't go on dinner dates and not eat."

7

"I think Jim stuffs her with rich foods deliberately," proclaimed Enid.

Janey batted her eyes.

Martha prepared a tray while Janey hung her topcoat in the hall closet.

When Janey and the tray had been placed before an east window, Martha stood back. "Now look at the view and forget what we've having and you'll make out."

Janey looked at the view. How thrilled she'd been her first night there. Imagine one Jane McBride living in a place like this. It was even more exciting than watching her first taped television appearance. Acres and acres of street lights gleamed like boxes of jewels.

"Bah," said Janey, and looked at the tray. One cup skimmed broth, one salad of raw vegetables and a blob of cottage cheese with an egg yolk grated over it, and for dessert, half a grapefruit. And *they* were having maple custard pie.

It wasn't worth it.

Behind her one voice was pitched too high. "She was perfectly contented until she met that Jim Rainey."

Contented? She'd been too busy to be anything else, or even to recognize the feeling. But who'd settle for contentment with stars popping up on the roadside and dandelions swinging from the sky? That was how she felt around Jim.

Ina, full of food and good will, came over to

8

commiserate. "Why don't you two marry? Then you won't have to stay twice as small as life."

"Can't for two years," murmured Janey. "You know Grandma can't get along on her pay. She has two years to go before Grandpa's annuities mature. Jim's having a tough enough time being the youngest man in that ad agency, without being saddled with a wife and a grandmother."

"You are in a bind. Guess you'll just have to whittle down and hold your job. Thank goodness I took up stenography; employers don't care what shape you're in."

If only it were as simple as that. With nothing but beauty as a qualification, where would she find a job that paid enough to keep her and help her grandmother?

On the other hand, how could she hold Jim's interest if she lived on lettuce and grapefruit and continued to look "like a two-armed road sign."

"Why?" she cried passionately, "doesn't someone invent a camera with a diminishing eye?"

Enid came over for the tray and nodded. "Tough. Looks like you're going to have to make a choice: your job or your fiancé. With your looks, a new fiancé would be easier to find."

She didn't want a new one. She had the only one she would ever want: long, rangy, blue-eyed, black-haired Jim Rainey, who could live on whipped cream, doughnuts and chocolates by the box without ever gaining an ounce, yet who wanted his beloved well padded with curves.

As for her looks: she'd been looking at the same face for the past twenty years. She imagined even the Taj Mahal would lose its luster if seen dozens of times a day over a span of years.

Her eyes were brown, her hair originally blond. Elaine insisted upon a rinse "tawny" brown; she said Janey looked gaudy in her original state.

What did she have that dozens hadn't? she wondered, donned a fetching robe and went in to find Enid entertaining an unexpected male guest, which meant she had to perch on a kitchen stool until he left.

Meanwhile her problem was unsolved. It was Jim versus her job. She brightened a little, thinking that if she lost her job there would be no problem. No pay, no food. But then she would have neither Jim nor pay, and what about Grandma?

Jim telephoned when she was at her lowest. Perched on the uncomfortable stool, she couldn't sound anything but what she felt: beat.

"Just what did you have for dinner?" he demanded, and added, "Don't say food. Now tell me."

Because it was impossible to lie when she looked into his stern blue eyes, and on the phone she always closed her eyes and imagined them, she told the truth.

"Are you trying to kill yourself?" he roared.

"Do you know what happens to girls who don't eat properly?"

"Umhum, they hold their jobs. Jim, don't you understand? Elaine gave me two weeks. I can either count it as my vacation or as my separation pay. But I must lose four pounds to make it a vacation."

"Hmmm," he buzzed, and because she couldn't see his eyes she didn't completely comprehend his next words.

"Tell you what. We'll build you up physically the first week, right? Then you go out to that beauty farm I've been telling you about and let them take off the excess. Stay off liquids the last couple of days and you can weigh in at Elaine's figure."

That night and the next morning she slept like a kitten, merely curling her paws when Martha, trying to be quiet, fell over an ottoman.

She awakened starved, and let herself go. Cream in her coffee, and three big jam-filled crullers. She eyed the fourth, but her capacity was limited.

She found the world a lovely place. She liked the rain still tearing past the windows. She couldn't go out and walk in that, could she? And she had a dinner date with Jim. In short, she had everything.

The girls remarked how vital she appeared, and she nodded. "I've been on a starch and carbohy-

11

drate bender," she explained. "I even ate those chocolate bits you bought for cookies, Martha."

"If it's worth the loss of your job—" muttered Martha.

"We'd better start looking for a new tenant," mourned Enid.

"Have fun," said Ina.

She had. Never had Jim been so approving. He even understood that she couldn't start out by eating as much as he. Her intake had shrunk. But each evening she could consume a little more, until by the end of the week she would be able to enjoy the same quantities as he.

"But, Jim," she wavered, "what will this enlarged capacity do when I start cutting down the second week?"

"We'll worry about that when the time comes. How about a new job? You type, don't you?"

"After a fashion. I learned in high school, but I could practice."

"Fine; I'll send up a typewriter. You can spend the mornings practicing."

Janey didn't sleep quite as late the next morning. She had to answer the doorbell and accept the typewriter Jim had sent up.

All of the time she was preparing a savory breakfast she floated around feeling tender toward Jim. Such thoughtfulness. He'd even tried to show her how they could marry on his present salary.

12

They could, of course, except for Grandma. He knew Grandma had done without a lot of things to rear Janey; it was only right Janey should see her through this difficult time.

She sat down at the table, the morning paper propped up before her. Someone, probably Enid, had left it open to the Help Wanted column, and right smack before her eyes was a list of Typists Wanted.

She felt a momentary elation at seeing how many were wanted. Then she looked at the salaries and understood why. A girl would have to live at home on those wages.

"Now is the time for all good men to come to the aid of their figures," typed Janey, and thought maybe if she married she could take such a job and still keep Grandma going for the next two years.

"When in the course of human events it becomes necessary," her fingers typed dutifully, "to rush home wornout and throw a halfway decent meal on the table and be cross like Martha and Enid and sometimes Ina—"

No, that would be starting married life with a handicap, and she was hungry. Maybe a bacon and tomato sandwich.

It was the next night Jim asked how she was coming with her typing.

"It's the typewriter," Janey complained. "It talks back. I start out with the Declaration of Independence, and it writes 'to dissolve matrimonial bonds' instead of political ones. And it's right. Maybe you'd be big enough to let me work to pay Grandma's rent, but I'd be feeling guilty and on the defensive."

"Have some more scalloped potatoes; they use real cream in these. And stop worrying."

She did right up to Saturday night. Of course one always weighed more at night, but when she was dressing to go out with Jim, she stepped on the scales and nearly fell into the bathtub.

Now she had ten pounds to shed in one week.

"Jim," she all but wept, "that's a pound a day. If I take a typist's job I'll be ready for a sideshow by Christmas."

"Don't be ridiculous," he retorted sharply. "You were starved. You're only building up to normal. You will level off in no time. If I didn't have to go on a three-week trip to agency head-quarters, we'd marry right away and worry about Grandma later."

At the moment she wasn't worrying about Grandma. For anyone as conscious of figures as Jim, he had a complete blind spot where financial figures were concerned. She had to live some place. She couldn't stay on with the girls on a typist's salary, providing she were efficient enough to find a typist's job.

She forgot some of this while going out to the airport with Jim. She remembered it riding back

14

in. Easter was not too far away; the slack season was about over. Elaine wouldn't wait; she'd find a new model to show her Easter creations.

"I simply must go out to that beauty farm while I still have money to take off what I put on."

The next morning Enid said she'd drive her out if she'd wait until evening, but Janey refused. Why lose eight hours when ten pounds were involved. An interstate bus passed within a quarter of a mile of the farm.

The interstate bus stopped at the right place. The driver said so. Janey, one wardrobe case, one overnight case and one beauty case were left to consider his words after the bus drove on.

"Well I can't just stand here," she said aloud, "not in this rain."

She had a choice of directions, and set forth due west, to be greeted by a herd of cows. By the time she had covered an equal distance due east, both she and her bags were dragging.

Ahead lay a valley, and arching it half a dozen rainbows. She counted them, decided she was delirious, and lunged on to find a man-made arch setting the pattern, beyond it an administration building like a brooding hen that had hatched out dozens of small replicas.

There seemed no one in the administration building when she entered; then she heard a noise, turned and saw a man as unbelievable as the rainbows.

"My goodness, you do need building up," he greeted her. "Give us a month and we'll have some flesh on that frame. Now here's the typewriter; if you're not too worn out, you can start on these menus."

Chapter Two

Had the desk not had a chair before it, Janey wouldn't have sat down. She would have turned out the door and started looking for a return bus.

"Be with you in a minute," said the male vision. "I'll turn the heat on in your cabin. You'd better rest before lunch; just dash off those—"

He departed. He also took her bags with him. Janey made one feeble effort to recapture them, then gave up.

So she needed building up? And they would have more pounds on her in a month? Maybe one lost the first week, then began taking it on the next three. As she had money enough and time enough for one week only, it might work.

But imagine being put to work! And on menus. Talk about cruelty to dieters. She had had only a cup of black coffee for breakfast.

Slyly she reached one hand for a menu, pulled it close and groaned.

"One med. T bone, quarter-inch butter melted on top. Two slices Provolo cheese. Leaf salad, oil, herb vinegar. Vanilla cream—"

She had read that far when she noticed there

was a name at the top. She was relieved. Imagine having such a meal set before one, then not eating it.

She leafed through other menus. Almost all had different items added or subtracted.

Removing coat and hat, she settled down, her fingers moving across the keys without a mistake. This was fun, but she was working up one whale of an appetite.

"Good girl!" The vision was back. "You're going to work out fine. I think you understood the terms: board according to your physical need; your own cabin plus utilities. Of course the salary doesn't amount to much, but considering what you gain in health—"

He broke off to stare at Janey. "You did understand, didn't you? We pay only thirty a week. Young lady, you are Dorothy Dunford, aren't you? You did talk to me over the telephone last week? You said you'd be here last Wednesday. No, you didn't!"

"I am Janey—"

He broke in right there. "You can't be. The man who telephoned your reservation said you had to remove four pounds."

"Ten," corrected Janey sadly.

"Young woman, do you know what happens to girls who insist on a slat-like figure?"

"They hold their jobs. I am a model."

"There are girls who can maintain a model's

figure without sacrificing their health. You're not one of them. The only thing I'd consent to do would be—" He hesitated.

"Restack me?" offered Janey hopefully, and thought of trying to restack ten pounds of butter where it wouldn't show.

Into the eyes of the handsome blond man came a light Janey had never seen before and didn't recognize as the flame of the zealot. Here was a man who'd restore health to his patrons if he put them in the poorhouse in the process.

Gracefully he swung around to sit on the edge of the desk. "I'll make a deal with you. I think the Dunford girl got as far as the bus stop, decided this was too lonely for her and went back to the city. If you'll take her place this week, we'll give our service free and charge you nothing for maintenance."

Janey almost stood up and cheered. All of this for nothing.

"And we'll pay the thirty dollars," he added as an extra inducement.

Half an hour later Janey teetered into Cabin No. 7. She had just saved a hundred dollars and earned thirty. And she had a bedroom with a bed in it. For one whole week she could retire without the gymnastics of letting down the bed divan, making the bed, then reversing the process in the morning. All this and a small sitting room with a view.

Janey looked at the view and shook her head. There were those rainbows again. This was all a dream or a hangover from that starch and carbohydrate bender.

Or was it? The vision had a name, Nick Larson. Soon she would meet the rest of the staff, from psychiatrist to dietician, and such guests as were present, this being the slack time of the year.

She had learned quite a bit about the farm in that half-hour. It wasn't maintained merely to remove or restack excess avoirdupois; that was the least of its concerns.

Larson said they had thought of calling the place the Open Door to a New Life. Tired businessmen, bored women, convalescents came to renew their health and with it found a fresh interest in living.

Janey thought that was all very fine, but what she wanted was a realignment so she'd be able to hold her job and keep on living the way she had been for two more years at least.

Thinking of this, she naturally thought of Jimmy. Men, she reasoned, were all alike. They turned for a second look at a slim girl, but wanted their own pleasingly plump. Now why?

"Ha," said Janey happily, "so the others won't turn for a second look. That proves Jimmy loves me."

She carried the thought right into the nap Nick Larson had ordered and wakened to find there was something wrong with it. By no stretch of the imagination could Larson be interested in her.

Nor she in him, she thought at noon, walking toward the big dining hall. There he stood, women of all ages clustered around him, the few men knotted about a figure Janey couldn't see just then.

The interior of the building was a complete surprise. It was filled with booths, some seating four, some six, some eight, and some only two or even one.

Janey was led to a booth for two.

In another moment a woman sidled in, propped up a book and, looking over the top, asked brightly, "Monoxide gas?"

Beauty farm? thought Janey hysterically. This was a loony bin. Look at the way she was devouring the pellets in a saucer: red ones, pink ones, a yellow and two olive green. Oh, they were vitamin pills, and she herself had a saucer of them. The woman was eying them hungrily.

"Ah-ah, not the two big ones," warned her companion; "they come after. Now then, don't you feel like the alphabet?"

Janey would have flown, but a waitress appeared, and right down before her placed the most beautiful steak she had ever seen, with butter. She'd eat that. It would give her strength to run.

"If you're not monoxide," the woman persisted, "what are you?"

"Irish," stated Janey firmly, and the woman burst into laughter.

"Forgive me," she bubbled. "We're assigned to tables with those suffering similar deficiencies bought on by similar causes."

"Oh," Janey's relief showed in her voice, "no, I'm overweight."

"You are what?" The woman's head shook as though to free it of illusions. "Goodness, and I thought I was cured." And back she went to her book.

Janey was sorry. She wanted to ask questions. She liked this big room, the tone and tune of it. Voices were muted, yet when one did rise it held a lilt of laughter.

From a table raised slightly on a dais, Nick Larson beamed down on her. Talk about Adonis, Rock Hudson and a dozen others all rolled into one, Nick beat all of them.

Having scraped the last of the meat from the steak bone, Janey sighed blissfully and attacked the salad, one eye on the high table. All but one person, a young person, a young woman, looked placid.

"Who is she?" Janey murmured.

Monoxide Gas didn't even look up. "Lola, athletic director of women. I think they should shift: give Nick the women and Lola the men. But then that would be poor strategy from a business angle."

22

Janey had gone from salad to cheese to a fruit gelatin with thick cream before she digested the remark.

"Oh," she said. Men would work with Lola with such zest they'd go tearing through the course, and women, trying to impress Nick, would do the same.

"The big pills now," ordered her companion. And because Janey didn't know whether she was talking to her or to herself, she obediently took the last in the box. "Calcium," continued the woman, "for the nerves, and Vitamin D. Now then, how did I do?"

For the first time she took her eyes from the printed page to scan the dishes, but Janey didn't wait. She supposed she'd been given this seat because she was an employee and wouldn't be scared off.

She meant to ask about the woman, but the moment she reached the administration building she was plunged into work, sorting code cards to file.

"Ever play solitaire?" inquired a voice.

It came from a man who resembled Jimmy, so she relaxed. Of course this man was older and had sandy hair, yet there was a certain something.

"Hours at a time," she replied solemnly. "Grandpa couldn't use his hands, so he used mine."

"About the same thing there. Names instead of suits and dates instead of numbers. That's how we check the improvement of our guests. Enjoy your lunch?"

"Oh my!"

"Janey, why do you want to lose weight?"

"So I can pay Grandma's rent," she replied.

Later, when she had identified her code letter, she would find the first notation "economic compulsion." After she had explained her two-year squirrel cage, she was surprised to find she had gone up in this man's estimation.

"It's good that you're engaged," he remarked thoughtfully.

"I think so too." She beamed. Then realizing he hadn't meant what she had, she said, "Oh, you mean because of Larson and the other women? Well, Jimmy may look like a hatrack wearing glasses, but he's —swell, he's—" She gave up.

The man belatedly said he was Dr. Campbell, observed thoughtfully that that wasn't exactly what he'd had in mind and, swinging off the desk, added something about harmony among staff members.

Janey shook her head and went back to work. Not only the guests here were a little "tetched."

Later, after she'd caught up on the cards, answered the telephone twenty times and made only fourteen mistakes in relaying the calls, she lifted her head from studying a brochure.

She tried to put the stilted phrases into her own words. Jimmy had called this a beauty farm. It called itself a health and beauty farm. Then what was she doing here? She wasn't sick.

Ah, but it was also a beauty farm.

She read another line: "Health and beauty are one, for who can be beautiful without health?" Janey could think of one. *Camille,* she reasoned, hadn't become a classic through bounding vitality. On the other hand, Camille hadn't had much fun out of her beauty.

Janey was working on another line, "Health and beauty are both physical and mental" when a second disembodied voice sounded. "I trust you brought proper clothing with you."

Janey whirled. It was the physical director, and there was no question about her physical beauty. She had black hair and eyes, red cheeks and lips and beautiful teeth. Now Janey knew the true meaning of a striking beauty. This one was coming at her, ready to strike.

"Proper?" Janey looked down at Elaine's conception of a business girl's dream.

"For walking. Those slippers!"

She'd paid a pretty penny for those slippers; they gave the exact tread a model needed.

"You will walk in the woods," explained the director. "That is part of your therapy."

Janey looked out to where rain now fell in a steady drizzle. "In weather like this?" she asked.

"You'll learn to enjoy it."

Not if I walk with you, thought Janey.

25

"One of our older guests is waiting. She knows the paths."

Monoxide Gas, thought Janey, and shivered. She didn't want to be caught in a lonely woods with that woman.

"We are sending you because you are an employee. You are not to talk. This woman can't bear the sound of a human voice. She's mentally sound but physically exhausted. She took over her sister-in-law's five children while the latter was having a nervous breakdown (she has three of her own) and collapsed the day her sister-in-law was discharged."

They were walking toward Janey's cabin for the required change of clothing. "Three television sets and eight children, and you know what this winter has been."

"No wonder she wants to be alone," breathed Janey compassionately.

"But she doesn't. She must have the solace of a guard who'll protect her from the sudden onslaught of noise. However, she's better. She's eating again."

"With eight children to feed, there wouldn't be much—"

"Oh, they had plenty of money; just a spare-the-rod discipline. It was when she tried taking her meals in the furnace room that her husband called in a psychiatrist. He found her purported idiosyncrasy an indication of normality."

26

Janey swallowed, then, at the cabin, held out a bronze hooded raincoat for Lola's inspection.

"I suppose it will have to do," murmured Lola. "But those shoes—"

Janey brought out bootees with built-in walkers to match the coat. Lola frowned, then turned on her professional smile. A thin, slightly haggard-looking woman was at the door, a slip of paper in her hand.

Lola waved at Janey and Janey nearly waved back, then with a dubious smile joined her nameless guest, and they went briskly into the rain.

It wasn't too bad. Janey was so busy trying to keep her breathing geared to their pace she hadn't time to worry over their silence. She even uttered a tiny, gasping "Whee" when her guide stopped at the top of the first hill.

From there they looked down on the valley with its half-moon of roofs, the health and beauty farm. Figures moved around. One dot in a scarlet sweater and little else was bobbing around on the tanbark circle beyond the cabins.

Her guide started down the other side, and belatedly Janey followed. Below lay a narrow canyon; alder catkins blushed rose above moss-green trunks and limbs. A stream came hurtling down the side of the farther mountain, made a great to-do of the direction it was supposed to take, then, with a frothy leap, accepted its destiny.

Janey breathed deeply and thought of the eve-

27

ning meal and Jimmy. Jimmy loved picnics and rivers and creeks and all kinds of wild things, from plants to mammals.

Jimmy had taught her—

Janey crammed both hands into her mouth. What did one do at a time like this? If she did what she felt like doing, she'd scream. But Lola had warned her: one violent sound and the guest would revert.

Out went a thin hand toward fuzzy green growth only half hiding a stand of waxy yellow Johnny-jump-ups. Down went the hand.

And the silence was shattered, but not by Janey. When the figure started to jump forward, she did give forth a warning: "Don't, or you'll spend your time with your feet in the air. They are nettles," she explained, hurrying down. "Oh, dear, and there's not a bottle of salad oil around."

The woman gave her the kind of look she had given Monoxide Gas. "I wasn't thinking of eating them," she snapped.

"One does, after they're cooked, I understand. But I meant soaking your hands in the oil eases the sting. It's about the only thing that does, Jimmy says."

"His name is Nick," corrected the woman.

"Oh, no, it isn't. My fiancé's name is Jim Rainey."

Now what had she said? The woman's expression had changed to one of delighted friendliness.

"Darling, how wonderful. Joe should have told me. Oh-oh, he couldn't. I'm not talking to him."

Talking was the key word. Janey, off in the woods a mile from help, looked at the woman who'd been taking her meals in the furnace room.

"I am not supposed to talk," she said stiffly.

"Oh, but you are. I've been dying to talk to someone, and now you're here we can have a ball discussing the strange people at the farm. You and I have so much in common."

Oh, dear, thought Janey.

"Jimmy's responsible for me being here, you know."

That did it. Janey turned back toward the trail, muttering something about salad oil, and the woman ran to catch up with her. Janey walked faster. So Jimmy hadn't been concerned about her figure; it was her mind he feared was slipping. Maybe he was right.

"My husband is Joe Stedman—" the woman raced right along with her— "your Jimmy's boss."

Chapter Three

When the path had been cleared a tree had had to be felled. The stump was still there. Janey collapsed on it and started to laugh.

"Move over," ordered Mrs. Stedman. "Isn't this ridiculous? I suppose Jimmy didn't tell you because of that no fraternizing among families of employees' rule."

Janey thought it more likely Jimmy had forgotten. She did dimly remember that back around the first of the year he'd mentioned that Stedman's wife was ill. And hadn't he mentioned family trouble?

He had. Mrs. Stedman promptly went into it. "This farm is so much more sensible than divorce," she said chattily. "Joe, like a lot of bighearted men, has a habit of dumping family and friends on me. This last was too much. Joe's sister doesn't believe in discipline, or punishment, as she calls it. Our own got out of hand when we had her five around, and I simply went under and stayed under. I," she informed Janey, "am in self-imposed exile. When I'm sure Joe has learned to restrain his hospitality, I'll stage a recovery."

"And the children?" asked Janey.

"They're old enough for boarding school. They are enjoying it. They too need a rest. Please, don't think I came here originally to escape. At that time I didn't care where I went, if any place. I was exhausted."

"Then you do like the farm?"

"There should be one in every community, a veritable halfway house that catches incipient conditions before they become acute. We'll go into that later," she added, glancing at her watch. "We'd better get back now, or they'll send someone after us. People do get lost."

They were a little breathless when they topped the hill, and Janey even more so when she saw the rainbows again.

"Too many of them," she complained.

"Probably only one; the others are reflections. Monoxide Gas—oh, you're at her table, aren't you? She tried to explain, but I couldn't grasp it."

Janey yearned to ask questions about her table mate.

"I'm still trying to understand why this is called a beauty farm. What, for instance, does Monoxide Gas want with beauty?"

"Oh, that. If you had a choice, which would you rather be—an old battle-scarred desk thrown on a junk wagon, or a well polished antique still in good use? I imagine you are thinking of

31

young girls. You'll find many here later in the season, especially during vacation time."

She said she had to rush back and dress. She believed she felt ready to join the guests in the dining room. And she was starved.

Come to think of it, so was Janey. She could hardly wait for the discreet buzz which announced the dining room was open.

A few guests were eying Mrs. Stedman with consternation. Mrs. Stedman was pouring oil on her hands instead of over her leaf salad. Janey set them at ease by asking if the nettle sting was still sharp. As she left, there was a buzz of talk, each of the four at the Stedman table contributing homeopathic remedies.

Janey even smiled at Monoxide Gas, but that worthy lady had her head low over a book. Janey beamed at the waitress who placed a bubbling cheese omelet before her, then almost forgot to eat it.

She could accept her tablemate's low, "These are not eggs," but when she said in the same dogged voice, "These are rice," Janey sputtered.

She managed a quick recovery with, "Interesting book?"

The woman looked up. "I wouldn't know," she sighed. "I wrote it twenty years ago. Imagine being driven to reading your own work to eat."

Janey swallowed. So this was an author. And here she spent spare moments dreaming of the day Jimmy would write a book. All advertising men wrote books, or hoped to. Well, from now on she'd keep his life so full there wouldn't be time to follow in the questionable footsteps of authors.

"Go on, eat your—"

"Rice?" offered Janey brightly.

"Thank you. For your sake, I should explain recovering one's taste is much like having feeling return to a numbed limb after serious injury. You know it is a sign of recovery, but the pain in unbearable. I try to become so absorbed in a book I won't realize I am eating."

Believing this woman was like a friend, so allergic to eggs she couldn't bear a hen's cackle, Janey made the proper comment.

She talked about Martha's pet casserole of rice, meat and cashew nuts until the last of the others' omelet had disappeared. And Janey's was cold.

Oh, well, anything for the cause, she thought brightly, and wondered when this beauty farm was going to take her particular case under consideration.

It did the next morning. Nick Larson came into the office and gave Janey such an impersonal look she wondered what mistake she had made. She caught several words and acted on them: gym and swim suit.

Lola provided the swim suit and chaperonage, also asides as Janey swiveled back and forth in her favorite model's walk.

"Take ten and what'll she have left?" inquired Lola in a carrying voice.

"One of the finest frames we've had here," Nick snapped back. He dismissed Lola and escorted Janey to a suite of offices at the rear of the gymnasium where a woman physician waited eagerly.

"With a little more sleep and a lot more food, we could use you as our health and beauty farm model," she beamed when she had given Janey an hour of her time and its equivalent in training.

Going on to the psychiatrist's office, Janey shook her head. Sleep and food. Imagine having all she wanted of each. Ah, but that was a luxury she couldn't afford.

Nick came into the office shortly before noon, and she blinked. Queer how he affected her just as the multiple rainbows did.

"Ran you through fast," he apologized, "because of the time you gave yourself. Now we can take off those pounds you call excess before the end of the week. But remember this: quick loss, quick gain. You know what that means."

Solemnly she nodded. "Starvation or setting up a home away from home out here. Recurrent fever sort of thing."

"Have you considered the strain that will be on you? Or does your job mean enough to offset it? Janey, exactly how do you feel about your work?

34

Would you, for instance, want to keep on with it indefinitely?"

If she lost Jim she'd have to. Then a second thought came. There was an age limit on modeling of her type. And one thing about age: it couldn't be banished even at this beauty farm.

What did they do with old models?

"I was born a hundred years too late," she replied gravely. "At my sorority we used to hold jam sessions on the future. We all wished we'd been born earlier. All our grandmothers had to worry about was doing what came naturally: marrying, caring for a home and family. But these days—"

Larson looked at her with fresh interest. "Go on."

"Well, these days, if one really works at a profession, there isn't time to find the right husband. Besides, you spend hours and days and months and years boning up for the big deal. And then you marry and don't carry on. Knowing and hoping you will marry, you never feel quite as a man does about a career."

"Well, isn't it worth-while to have a profession to fall back on if anything happens to your husband and you're left to support a family?"

"It sounds good, but try to get back after you've been out ten or fifteen years. The profession you've learned has developed a lot of new angles."

"Speaking of angles," Larson said, "how about this weight removal? You can have a steady job

35

here as long as you want it. When you take your noon break, sit down at your desk in the cabin and add up what you'll really be making here; then compare it with your modeling job and see which you really prefer."

Janey approached her noon meal like a convict his last supper. Fortunately, it was liver. And amazingly, Monoxide Gas was eating it with relish and without a book.

"I wouldn't touch it when I was normal," she said brightly, and added, seeing the expression on Janey's face, "No association."

"Oh," said Janey.

In her cabin she dutifully jotted down the costs of living with the girls and subtracted them from her salary at Elaine's.

It just didn't seem possible there could be more money from less pay until she remembered she'd been paying quite a lot back to Elaine for clothes she needed to hold her job there.

"What did you decide?" Larson asked when she returned to the office.

"It was the liver," she began apologetically, then wondered if he intended to take her temperature. "I mean at lunch. I remembered why I didn't like it.

"The only time Grandpa ever took me to the woodshed we'd had liver for lunch. I gagged. He whipped me because I had promised the Sunday School superintendent I'd carry notice to the local paper. I'd forgotten and caused a lot of people a lot of trouble. The whipping and the liver went together, reminding me I must always keep a promise."

She looked so wistful Nick Larson might have made some manly gesture of reassurance had he not seen Lola approaching.

"Yet you'd rather be here. Tell you what. I'll find some temporary help, and any time you find your scales going up, you come right out here and we'll bring them down again. Right?"

Lola entered with all of the poise of a mother hen calling her duckling back from dangerous waters. She grew affable when Nick told her Janey felt she must return to Elaine's because she'd had liver. Then he beat a hasty retreat, leaving the liver literally in Janey's lap.

"Now then," Lola held a slip of paper in her hand, "we must set about preparing you for your position in a forthright manner."

Janey had a distinct impression that, given her "rathers," Lola would have set about whittling off the excess. Her method the next morning was nearly as painful.

Bruised and feeling broken, Janey pulled herself from bed, then sat up, horrified. She'd had a date with Jim's boss's wife. Here she'd had a chance to cement friendly relations, create a smooth path for Jim's (and her own) future, and she'd let Lola ruin it.

But she hadn't. Janey was still on the edge of the bed when Mrs. Stedman came in, bright-eyed and laughing. "You poor duck, Lola is certainly giving you the worst possible impression of the beauty farm. But cheer up. The whole staff jumped her publicly. Campbell swore the way she drove you around the ring, whiplashing you, was pure sadism, and when Larson learned she hadn't sent you to the steam room afterwards, my, oh my."

"Oh dear," cried Janey. There went her job in the hole.

"Then," continued Mrs. Stedman with relish, "Monoxide Gas tied it up with a pink bow. She said in a lofty tone, 'One would think Miss Lansing jealous of the little model.'"

"That really did tie it," Janey moaned. "Now Lola will hate me."

"Cheer up; she'd have hated you anyway. Monoxide just brought it out in the open. From now on little Lola will be afraid to be anything but decent to you. Her type can't allow anyone to believe she fears anything."

Fears? thought Janey.

"Jealousy is fear, you know. Now about food —You missed dinner last night."

"I didn't want any. Lola brought me a tray with half a grapefruit and a bouquet of lettuce leaves. Sometimes I wonder if it's worth it."

"It isn't," Mrs. Stedman told her soberly.

38

"Whenever you have to sacrifice your health to the demands even of someone you love, it isn't worth it to either one of you. Believe me, I know."

Janey, being late for breakfast, found a tray delivered to the office. Contents: one raw egg beaten into one glass of orange juice. But there was a promise of a glass of milk in four hours.

Not that the day was altogether dark. Larson came in, beaming. Monoxide Gas was making a remarkable recovery and crediting Janey. Watching Janey's enjoyment of food had been an inspiration. As for Mrs. Stedman, she had broken the sound barrier, a great advertisement for the beauty farm.

"We could increase your salary in the summer months," he offered.

A letter from Jimmy brought both joy and concern. Hearing from him was wonderful, but when she caught a glimpse of herself in a darkened windowpane she groaned. And this was only the beginning. By the time he returned she'd look like a coat hanger with hair.

Lola, crisply efficient, sought to make up for her treatment of the previous day by suggesting a hike, alone, in place of a tanbark trot.

She said she had assumed Janey had enough intelligence to go to the steam room after such a workout, and Janey held her fire. For hadn't Lola said, "Now go to your cabin immediately"?

Dutifully Janey trotted down a graveled road,

then felt her spirits soar. Directly ahead there were clouds massed on a mountainous horizon "like whipped cream piped around a blueberry pie," she cried.

"And smack dab in the middle a mound of ice cream." She knew it was Mt. St. Helens, and she couldn't think of a nicer compliment.

Seeing something white in the woods, she fell over a few low shrubs and two rotten logs. But it was worth it. She counted eighteen trilliums when she reached the glade. Wouldn't Jimmy love this?

Trotting back was more difficult. It was uphill, and with nothing but a glass of orange juice ahead as an inducement, her ankles faltered. Then clouds parted as she reached a bend, and there stood Mt. Hood, a triangle of gold almost within reach of her hand, despite its eleven-thousand foot height.

That settled it. Jimmy must come to the farm for his vacation. She'd arrange to take hers at the same time, take him out to such beauty spots as this. And then she remembered she was having all of the vacation she was going to have.

By the time she reached the top of the hill she had lost her breath. She recovered it, slipped into the steam room, lost it again, then recovered it with a howl under an icy shower.

But she felt wonderful right up to the moment she met a waitress with a tray holding one glass of

40

orange juice with two eggs as beat up as she felt looking at them.

Almost as devastating to her morale as the absence of food was isolation from the dining room. She liked people. She thought of going to the big recreation hall with its glass walls, giant fireplaces, booknooks and game corners, but that hall came equipped with television sets. She might close her eyes to the commercials, but unless she wore ear plugs she'd be tantalized by adjectives.

Morning brought one cup of black coffee and a rusk. Nick Larson watched anxiously as Janey crossed to the administration building.

"How do you feel?" he asked.

"Slinky," she replied, and elucidated, "I could model leotards this morning."

"I am afraid I'm beginning to agree with your fiancé," Larson commented unhappily. Then abruptly, "Mail's in."

All though the early sorting of the mail Janey considered his words. When the two most wonderful men she had ever met preferred her in her natural state, why did she punish herself to remain unnatural to hold a job?

Now what? asked Janey of Janey, for she had uncovered an envelope addressed to her in a well known hand, her grandmother's. And Grandma never wrote when she could telephone unless she was in trouble.

Chapter Four

Grandma McBride was in trouble all right. The moment Janey opened the letter and found a different handwriting within, she feared the worst. Grandma kept an emergency envelope addressed to Janey, to be used if she were unable to write or speak.

She was unable to write. Janey's mouth and eyes grew round as she read the neighbor's report of what had happened.

Young Michael O'Mahoney had a scooter. He also had a bad habit of leaving it in dark thoroughfares. All of his parents' friends and relatives knew of his weakness and guarded against it, principally by keeping away from the O'Mahoney home. Baby sitters had also kept away from the home until, in desperation, the parents combed the next town and found Grandma. And Grandma had found the scooter.

"She said it wouldn't have been so bad if the front door hadn't been open," wrote the neighbor. "She just pretended she was on one ski up to there. But as there had been no snow on the terrace she lost her balance at the threshold and went down, trying to ease the impact with both hands. It was a brick terrace."

For the first half-hour after reading the letter, Janey could only think of Grandma and the pain she must have suffered. One split wrist was bad enough, but two must be unbearable. Why hadn't they called her?

Suddenly she realized Grandma must be in a hospital. Again she scanned the letter. Grandma, thank goodness, had insurance to cover her expenses. Not that Janey wouldn't have given her every cent she possessed, but a new cloud was rapidly rising on her horizon.

Grandma's baby sitting had provided her with food and utilities. Not even Grandma could baby sit without both hands in swift working order. Now she, Janey, would have to Grandma sit.

What am I going to do? she whimpered inwardly.

The beauty farm job was out. She'd not only have to keep slimmed down to Elaine's figures but do a little finagling on the side. The girls would cover for her, she was sure. She'd find the cheapest cottage in town, then have messages relayed through the girls. Elaine need not know she had moved.

What else could she do? Grandma wouldn't part with her furniture. It was all she had left of Grandpa, she insisted. It was cheaper to use it than to store it.

Another horrifying thought concerned Grandma's cooking. How could she maintain her model weight with Grandma in the kitchen?

Guests came in for their mail, and as both Nick and Lola were busy elsewhere, Janey passed it out. She was unaware of the picture she presented or the buzz of talk she inspired.

The buzz reached the ears of Nick Larson. Up went his handsome head, back went his shoulders, and off strode Nick to the dietician to order a substantial lunch for Janey.

The buzz also reached the ears of Dr. Campbell. Thoughtfully he strode over to Janey's office, thoughtfully caressed his chin and murmured, "Quarrel with the young man?"

"Oh, no, he's in Chicago. No," she sighed deeply, "Grandma can't sit any more." She saw his look of shock. "Baby sit," she hastened to say, then went into the story of her accident.

"Your grandmother loves children?" he asked.

"Can't abide them."

"Aha!" he leaped at the words. "Sublimation. The accident, I mean."

"Don't you mean escape?" asked Janey bravely.

"No. If this young Michael is the way he sounds, your grandmother sublimated her desire to murder him by trying to kill herself."

"Oh." It was a bit difficult to imagine Grandma wanting to murder anyone. Feeling she had given a wrong impression, Janey sought to cover up.

44

"Baby sitters aren't allowed to discipline their charges, and the older children take out their repressed desires to raise cain on the sitter. Besides, she only took up that vocation as a last resort."

"I see. And what is her real desire? Has she a hobby?"

"Weeds."

"Weeds," he echoed. *Weeds?*

"Before Grandpa died she made beautiful pictures with them. She used weeds and stalks and things, but the frames cost so much she had to stop giving them as presents!"

"Weeds," murmured Campbell, then brightened. "At least she chose something with no intrinsic value. On the other hand, speaking of hands—" He stopped right there. What would a woman do without the use of her hands?

"And I must be bright and cheerful and full of plans when I run up to visit her," she mourned aloud.

Questioning was the good man's business. Before he was through he knew more about Janey and Grandma McBride than they knew. And he comforted Janey on one score. Someone from the farm would drive her up-river for the visit.

A stiffly antagonistic Lola relieved Janey at noon. By then Janey was eager for even the egg and orange juice, but when she reached her cabin no food was there.

Eventually Nick Larson came in, and he too

seemed angry when he learned she had not been told to report to the dining room.

She didn't care, for awaiting her there was a steak, a big beautiful piece of cheese and her favorite salad: mandarin orange sections and avocado. And if one waitress looked smug and one guest trying to gain weight looked askance at the salad she had been served, Janey didn't notice.

Everyone seemed to have heard of Grandma's accident. All came to offer commiserations and the use of their cars and their driving, leaving Janey in the difficult position of having to choose until Nick informed them all that he had business at the Dalles and would take Miss McBride to the hospital.

It was almost too much. Janey ate and beamed and looked joyfully at dessert: jello with what looked like whipped cream.

" 'Abstinence makes the appetite grow stronger,' " misquoted Monoxide Gas, stopping at her booth. "Are you a good cook, Janey?"

Now what had she said? Sunshine and eagerness drained from Janey. Cook. Kitchen. And she'd been mean enough to worry about her figure with Grandma at the kitchen stove. Whoever heard of anyone cooking with splints on both hands?

"I'll have to feed her too," she replied thoughtfully, "and maybe fix up especially appetizing dishes to coax back her appetite. I am in a bind."

"Fine," beamed the woman. "Admitting it, I mean. You've faced the fact you're in trouble; hence you'll find a way out. Ever notice how many turn their backs on their problems, then wonder why they can't see a solution?"

Janey felt better. Possibly food, as well as the warm reception the guests had given, helped. Not even the sight of Lola striding down the path directly toward her dimmed her glow.

"I," Lola stated, "am going with you. You'll have to wait until I've had my lunch." And on she strode.

But Lola was wrong. Dr. Campbell drove up to announce he was the chauffeur.

"Because of relations between board members?" Janey asked.

"Well, yes. And then again, no. I have a faster car, and chains. We'll go over the hump and cut off a couple of hundred miles; have you home in time for dinner."

Janey didn't particularly mind. It would have been fun going off into the early spring with a man like Nick Larson, but if he came equipped with Lola as a chaperone, she'd settle for the doctor.

And it was a delightful drive. Once, after the chains were on, they cozily nudged Mt. Hood well above his snow line. And the weather remained clear enough for them to look down on the mighty Columbia curling its blue length below.

Janey had one awful moment as she and Dr. Campbell followed a fleet and silent-footed nurse along a dusky corridor of the hospital. She tried to dredge up all of the optimism she didn't feel and longed for Jimmy's staunch presence.

Then they were admitted to a room, and there sat Grandma McBride, looking like a kitten that had just lapped up the morning coffee cream: smug and guilty.

"Ah-*ha!*" came from Dr. Campbell, and Janey's head swam around in a circle. Now why that tone of triumph?

When her chauffeur was introduced, as a doctor, Grandma McBride jumped to conclusions. Beauty farm indeed! Why hadn't she written she'd been ill? Why hadn't Jimmy?

"Jimmy's in Chicago," Janey managed.

"Well, I've got a good mind to get out of this bed and go home with you, cook you some decent food. What you need—"

Then she became aware of her hands, and the expression Janey had anticipated on arrival crossed her face.

"Here I sat having the time of my life," she moaned, "resting, with expenses paid, and never a thought of what it would mean to you, Janey."

"Now now," soothed Campbell, all but licking his lips with satisfaction, "what your grandmother needs is—" he hesitated, then looked bright, "ice cream. I saw a store across the street."

Janey was in the elevator before she realized how adroitly Campbell had rid himself of a third person.

Later she didn't know whether it was the ice cream, her presence, or whatever Dr. Campbell had said in her absence, but something had cheered the senior McBride.

"What did you talk about?" she asked abruptly when they drove off. "I must know so I won't spoil it."

"Talk about? Oh, furniture."

"Furniture!" gasped Janey.

"She's been carrying seven rooms of furniture on her back for five years. You didn't help her shift the burden."

"Why I—"

"You agreed with everything she said. I didn't. I gave her a good excuse to be rid of it and, incidentally, to move out of that small ghost town. She feels 'let out of jail.' "

Janey was so disturbed at having Grandma on the loose she didn't protest when Campbell suggested they have dinner at a wayside place famous for its cuisine. She worked her way through half a fried chicken, French fried potatoes, and huckleberry pie with ice cream, with never a thought of Elaine or her job.

Grandma at home, plus furniture, was a known

expense, X number of dollars per month. She even had enough, thanks to the beauty farm, to see her through until her hands mended enough to take on further baby sitting. But now—

"I suppose," she said bitterly, when they were back in the car, "you two planned where she'll go."

"No, that would spoil the fun. She has another week in the hospital, then two in a convalescent home. She'll have a ball making and discarding plans. Let her have her fun."

He talked quite seriously as they drove on. People were so intent upon living tomorrow they never enjoyed a moment of today. How far ahead did she live?

"Two years," murmured Janey absently.

"Like your grandmother. Now you think you can't marry for two years, and you go around feeling miserable. Has it never occurred to you that you might find someone more fascinating than your current fiancé in that time?"

"More fascinating than Jimmy?" cried Janey. "Impossible."

"It's barely possible part of the luster on both sides is that of the unattainable, the apple dangling just out of reach."

Ridiculous, stormed Janey inwardly, then looked down on the camp as they turned onto the side road. How lovely it looked at night, sparkling with lights. And she had to leave day after tomorrow.

Janey slept, but restlessly, and awakened with a deep sense of guilt. Within three weeks she would have a footloose grandmother on her hands. How could she coordinate her life at Elaine's with Grandma McBride?

Elaine's. Janey jumped out of bed. The food she had eaten yesterday! She'd be up in poundage to such an extent she wouldn't have that necessary job.

Queer, the scales said she was down.

Janey ignored the breakfast buzzer. Sternly she marched to the office and began the day's work, unaware of a second buzz, this of low-voiced conversation in the big hall. Janey had become a *cause célèbre*. She was being starved by Lola so she'd be sure Janey's job in the city was secure. Well, they'd fix that.

Surreptitiously buttered rolls, sweet rolls, even pancakes with sausage rolled inside went into handbags or pockets.

Monoxide Gas looked long and lovingly at a large piece of pink ham, golden brown on the edges, sighed, rolled it up and stuck it in her pocket.

Janey was alone at mail call. She thought it a bit strange that each guest came in alone; usually they came in couples or threesomes or foursomes, all talking at once.

51

She thought it strange until small napkin-wrapped packages were slipped across the counter to her. She did not have time to unwrap them. Twenty guests, one at a time, took up a large part of the morning.

When she did, eventually, she found a strange assortment of food spread out before her. And all she wanted yearningly was a cup of strong black coffee.

"Janey," Nick Larson would choose that moment to swing in with his light step, "what on earth? Ah, how many?"

He counted them. Twenty. One for every guest.

"Do you know what this means?" he demanded.

Woefully she looked up. "But, Nick, I didn't ask for anything or say anything or—"

"That is the wonder of it. Our guests thought so much of you they shared or even gave up the choicest part of their breakfasts. As they are all now at the point of being ravenous, that is self-sacrifice, even love."

"Oh," murmured Janey, "why didn't any of them long for black coffee?"

"Poor child. Be right with you."

Lola would come in just as they'd dipped their heads to the fragrant brew, and Lola looked too dejected to care. Something was wrong, she informed them, and gave Janey a suspicious glance. The guests were turning against her. They were no longer friendly. Someone had started a whispering campaign.

It was then she saw the food, still spread on its napkins. "No wonder I can't reduce this girl to her proper weight. She doesn't want to return to her position. Well, I shall telephone Elaine and explain our failure."

"You will do no such thing," Nick informed her. "Had Janey been eating, the food wouldn't be there for you to see. She's now below the required weight level. Tomorrow I shall take her into Elaine's."

"I shall go with you."

"I," Nick stated firmly, "am taking the small car. It will carry only three. I am delivering Mrs. Stedman en route."

How to win friends, thought Janey dolefully as Lola stalked out.

Janey was quite surprised to learn Monoxide Gas, whose other name was Sally Stearns, would succeed her in the beauty farm office. "Better for the farm than putting her in a strait-jacket," Nick reported absently. "I mean she's one of those unfortunates who must have something to do to stay happy."

Mrs. Stedman, coming in with her bags the next morning, gave a different report. Monoxide had learned Lola had a friend picked out for the job and felt it should be kept open for "eventualities."

"Whatever they are," mourned Janey, and went

out to bid the farm farewell. It was a lovely morning, with sun shining on wet sword fern, with clouds bumping around the sky like toy balloons, and the scents of every known perfume of mountain and woodland.

She parted from the guests at mail call, thanked them collectively for wanting to give her a farewell banquet and begged them to realize Lola had been right in vetoing that. She really needed her job at Elaine's.

They had a happy drive in, dropping Mrs. Stedman at her home. Wistfully Janey looked at the split-level and said she and Jimmy would be delighted to spend a weekend there on his return. Some day, she thought, she and Jimmy would have such a home; a blissful thought until she remembered the furnace room where someone had taken her meals.

"But then neither Jimmy nor I have sisters or brothers," she said aloud, and Nick almost ran into a bridge guard rail.

"Oh, well, don't let that worry you. I intended talking to your Elaine for you," he misinterpreted. When she tried to beg him to keep out of her business relationships, he became masterful. She was one little girl who needed help.

So did he before he was through with Elaine. Not that the traffic court judge wasn't lenient. His wife had a charge account there; no one knew better how much time could elapse within the salon walls.

But that was later. Janey, skipping in a side entrance, caught a last glimpse of Nick Larson, head up, hat at the precise angle to set any woman's heart to slipping, striding into the salon.

When Janey started in from the opposite direction she found a knot of employees clustered behind the drapes.

"Look at her," whispered one, "all lit up like an electronic computer."

Unable to look over, Janey burrowed through, to see Elaine facing Nick Larson. Maybe it was Elaine's movements, the flash of salon lights on costume jewelry, but something established communication between those two. To Janey it meant only that she was stuck with her job, the one she had to keep and didn't want. Nick had really seen to that.

Chapter Five

It was impossible for the listeners to hear what was said between Elaine and Nick Larson. Elaine, lights still flashing, led him to her office.

Naturally attention swung to Janey.

"Imagine being around that for a whole week. Janey, what happened? He's out of this world."

"Umhum, and I'm in it."

"Janey, how much does it cost to get yourself planted on this farm?"

Relieved at the change in the subject, Janey answered as best she could. The fees depended upon the condition of the plant; that is, the person.

For a simple little overweight problem like hers one could get by on a couple hundred a week. That included room and board and ordinarily *why* you gained when you shouldn't.

"Who needs to know that?" scoffed one.

"You mean it's not all calories? I don't have to feel I'm punching an adding machine every time I put a bite in my mouth?"

She would have enjoyed telling the girls all of the beauty farm's secrets for a charmed life, but she didn't know them.

Fortunately, Elaine's secretary caused a diversion. Janey was to "pop into the salmon lamé and waddle into Elaine's august presence."

"Not that," she pleaded.

"Get a shoehorn," moaned another.

"I know Nick isn't interested in—"

"So does she, chick, but name me one other stretch of cloth more revealing."

"My hair is icky."

"Who'll look at your hair?"

Janey felt she was placing her grandmother's rent, livelihood and future in the hands of the dresser. She knew the fatal salmon-colored gown so well. It slipped on easily, fitted smoothly at the proper spots and allowed her to take two tiny steps at a time without pausing to realign the matching spike-heeled sandals.

Cautiously Janey trickled into Elaine's presence. Yes, she was looking like an IBM, lights flicking here and there. Then she looked at Nick Larson.

"I only hope," he said between set teeth, "nobody yells *fire* while she's trapped in that."

"You men," Elaine laughed happily, turned a severe look on Janey and flicked a hand in dismissal.

While there was nothing Janey would have enjoyed more than running to the nearest exit, she had to two-step out and thus heard the sudden

57

crisp note in Elaine's voice. "Now are we ready to talk business?"

Janey felt an impulse to swivel back and tell Nick she didn't want this gown, if that were what Elaine was trying to sell, then heard his reply.

"I'm admitting you can create the illusion of beauty. Our business is based upon an entirely different quality."

And that was all she heard. Later, the secretary slipped her a note telling her to report for work as usual Monday morning. She assumed this was a dismissal for that afternoon and wondered what to do about Nick.

He'd been nice enough to drive her to the city, though he'd also delivered Mrs. Stedman en route. And he'd said he wanted to talk to Elaine; from what she'd heard there was some business venture building between the two.

She admitted she had hoped he'd stay in town and they'd have the evening together. Such a beautiful spring evening, and Jimmy was so far away.

It wouldn't hurt just to happen to be passing by when he left the salon for his car.

Janey sped around the block to where his car had been left. Unhappily it was gone, and there was no one to tell her it now reposed in the police garage waiting to be bought out of hock. She blamed herself for spending extra time before the mirror.

Wearily she made her way toward the apartment. Ted would deliver her bags, save her cab fare. A surface car this time of the day gave her a feeling of doing right by her grandmother.

This was Saturday; the girls would be home. They were in the throes of preparations for a party. Seeing Janey, Martha wailed, "She'll make thirteen."

They tried to cover up but couldn't, especially after Janey had gone to the hall closet to find it bare, awaiting the topcoats of the coming guests.

She tried to cover up with a story of a late date which they were eager to accept. She also told them she would be leaving them just as soon as her grandmother could be left alone in an apartment, then had to hurry and explain it was her hands, not her brain, which were being mended.

She left immediately, arranged to have her bags held at the desk until the next day, then went to a corner of the lounge to consider her dilemma.

The girls weren't going to try to replace her. Each now had a steady date. They had found that thinking of Janey sitting it out on a kitchen stool cramped their style.

Janey had dinner at a neighborhood café and spent the hour thinking of the beauty farm, longing even for Monoxide Gas across from her uttering zany remarks. Then she toured the foyers of all the motion picture houses, found she'd seen all the pictures, bought a newspaper and learned such other pictures as she hadn't seen were at Drive-ins.

Returning to the apartment lounge, she found a secluded corner and wrote Jimmy a note, signing herself, "A displaced person." In trying to find a short cut to the desk, she came to a cul-de-sac of bookcases filled with old but unused books.

There was a window seat with a drop light overhead. Janey looked at her watch, counted the hours and settled down to Mrs. Gaskell's *Cranford*.

The manager, making his official check on the night crew, noticed the particular light burning, investigated and called his wife.

"It's all right," Janey insisted. "I made thirteen, so I'm just sitting it out down here until the other guests leave."

Assured the only guests who hadn't left hadn't arrived yet, it being nearly daylight, Janey accompanied Ed and Edna Mayer back to their apartment and was bedded down cozily in their guest room.

She tried to explain "the girls." The Mayers were not to blame them. It was like wearing a too tight dress all day. You got by, but once you had loosened the belt it was almost impossible to tighten it again. She had made the apartment too tight by her presence. They had lived together cheerfully until she had "loosened the belt" by going away for a week.

Mr. Mayer said that was one way to put it, but what did Janey intend to do?

They took that up at breakfast, Sunday morning breakfast, with layers of golden brown griddle cakes soaked in butter and syrup. So intent was Janey upon telling them about Grandma, she failed to count calories and had worked her way through two stacks before the shadow of Elaine fell across the sunshine of her appetite.

Well, she'd just have to starve the rest of the day. Yet how could she, with "the girls" so contrite they plied her with leftovers from the previous night's feast?

Telling them it was her own fault didn't soothe them; the only thing she could do was eat. So she ate.

Food, she thought, going down in the elevator to the room she would be using for the next two weeks, was a curious commodity. People used it to express concern or affection. Think of the way Jimmy ordered meals for her, soup to celery stalk one song of love. To refuse any of her wonderful friends was to rebuff their love.

To fail to refuse, she reminded herself, was to lose the job she'd barely retrieved.

The problem remained with her the next day. Mrs. Mayer wakened her with a gay good morning and a footed bed tray on which reposed one pot of coffee and one large bowl of steaming cereal, with cream and honey. It wasn't the sort of thing one could throw back into the face of the donor. She would have black coffee for lunch, nothing more.

In mid-morning Elaine herself brought Janey into the outer salon where one Mrs. Joseph Stedman and two friends of equal importance and high credit rating awaited her.

"Take all of the time you want," sang Elaine, waving them out at one o'clock. They did. They were convinced they had paid well for the little model's time with their morning purchases; now to inspect her across a luncheon table.

"I know what it is," cried the older of Mrs. Stedman's companions. "She makes one want to take care of her. That's what brought you out, Edie; you became so concerned with her."

"I do believe you're right," mused the younger. "Here, dear, these bite-sized biscuits won't add the shadow of an ounce—"

Martha telephoned at four-thirty. She was preparing Janey's favorite beef-cashew casserole; they'd expect her at six.

Janey tottered out of her former apartment, feeling deliciously full but dolefully guilty. One day back at work and she'd ingested more calories than she'd normally consume in a week. And the very people who ordinarily watched her weight had urged her on.

A special delivery letter from Jimmy climaxed a near-perfect day. "Old Joe" (Stedman) had telephoned him, raved about his fiancée, gave her credit for returning his wife to him.

"They're all crazy," said Janey happily, and read on.

Old Joe was going to do something for Jimmy. He didn't know what, but he didn't want Jim to lose a girl like Janey for lack of income.

But Jimmy hadn't heard about Grandmother yet. She hadn't wanted to worry him.

"Isn't he beautiful?" she asked Mrs. Mayer, who came in with a bedtime snack of "health cookies" and milk.

Mrs. Mayer looked at the photograph of a young man with a long face, horn-rimmed glasses framing near-sighted eyes, and lied like a landlady. "Just beautiful," she agreed.

She was in the kitchen before she conceded there was something about Janey's Jimmy.

Janey sat nibbling cookies—black strap molasses, chopped nuts, dates, raisins held together by oatmeal and, though she didn't know it, butter. There was something soothingly safe about the adjective "health," so she ate them all and awakened the next morning bursting with energy.

It was one of the nicest weeks Janey had lived since childhood. For once everybody, even Elaine, approved of her. Guests at the beauty farm were sending friends to the salon to meet Janey, and they were staying to buy from Elaine and invariably inviting her out to lunch or dinner.

When Mrs. Mayer wasn't concocting something with a health prefix, Martha or one of the other girls was remembering a dish Janey had particularly enjoyed.

Jimmy was getting along in his business, Grandma was getting along at the hospital, and Janey didn't have a single decision hanging over her head. Right up until Saturday forenoon, when who should appear but Nick Larson and Lola?

Of course any woman could have told Nick he should not have raved about that salmon-colored lamé. His saying it was atrocious would have been enough, but he had had to go into details.

Lola wasn't vain, merely realistic. She had a warm, dark beauty which would make the most of the salmon color. And she had, she knew beyond the shadow of a doubt, a much better figure than that little Janey person.

After a week of hearing Nick rave about that awful gown, first to one, then to another of the staff, and finally to guests, she knew she had to do something. She had to erase the picture of Janey by superimposing upon it one of herself in the same gown. She'd buy the darned thing if it took all of her savings.

"Operation shoehorn," sang out the dresser, signalling Janey. "Don't faint; someone really wants to buy that lamé. Up and in it, gal."

"Then let me give my best to it," sighed Janey.

"The sooner that moves out of Elaine's, the safer I'm going to feel. It has a certain something."

Or was it Janey who had a certain something?

"Kid, you've sure been living on the fat of the land this week. I can't squeeze you in."

Janey turned to the mirror, stared at the vision and groaned. Why, she wondered aloud, did it always settle in one spot?

"Well," Elaine swept in, "what is holding—" She stopped short, gave an exclamation which was composed of triumph, self-justification and some other ingredient. "Just walk right in here after me," she ordered Janey. "Yes, as you are, unzipped."

Janey didn't make her usual undulating entrance. She couldn't. Elaine was moving much too rapidly for the gown Janey wore, and she held Janey's left hand. Janey's right hand was still across her torso, trying to do something about the now jammed zipper.

"There, Mr. Larson," she heard Elaine say; "this explains better than words."

Janey saw both Lola and Nick at the same time, but her glance rested longer on Nick. He was nodding as though with inner satisfaction. "It explains you do not allow for normal expansion and contraction," he reproved her.

"With this model, only expansion is normal. She must go."

After that, Janey couldn't believe her ears.

Nick was saying, "Naturally," and Lola, of all persons, was leaping to her defense.

Janey missed the best of the battle. Elaine dismissed her, told her to report to the office later. She had been given her chance. This time, she would receive only one week's separation pay.

Janey carried the thought into the dressing room. Somehow she was making money on this. She'd paid the girls until the first, so Mrs. Mayer refused money for her guest room. Everybody had had a hand in feeding her. She'd earned thirty dollars at the beauty farm, and now she was to have, aside from this week's pay, one whole week of separation pay. She was doing all right up to now.

Of course she had lost her job.

Lola, slipping in, contrite because her desire to show Nick how she could look in that fool gown had cost Janey her job, caught Janey's doleful mood. Lola attempted to repair the damage she'd done.

"Don't move until you hear from me," she said firmly, and went out faster than she'd entered.

Janey wasted another few moments trying to work up a worry. Had Lola meant move as in move the body, or move as in leave one place of residence for another? If the former, she was going to have to have help with the zipper; if the latter, she'd already moved.

Something had happened to the dresser and the saleswomen who usually gathered at a time like this. Janey, who could think much better sitting down couldn't.

Word explosion sounded from the corridor. The dresser came in, skidded, stopped, drew from its safety pocket a pair of sharply pointed scissors and advanced upon Janey.

"I've had enough!" she announced.

Janey debated running, but that was impossible.

"This frock, this creation," the scissors were aimed just north of Janey's heart, "has been Elaine's torture garment too long." The scissors came down, reached the tight upper edge of the gown and clashed due east.

Janey's breath came out in a long, luxurious sigh, before she caught the import of the dresser's remarks.

Elaine, had made some kind of a deal with Nick Larson in which she, Janey, was involved. Nick hadn't had a chance, because Elaine would use this frock as she'd used it in time past to gain her own ends.

"But what ends?" asked Janey.

Chapter Six

The dresser gathered up the long, iridescent scales of the dead gown, scowling.

"I don't know what," she reported absently. "I do know Elaine had your successor picked out weeks ago and has been training her on the side. She brings with her entree to the Hunt Club set."

Janey sank into a chair. She should have been indignant. She wasn't, probably because she knew she hadn't been the one to fail.

"Then this Mr. Larson brings you back. He makes an issue of Elaine hiring you again. He will send business to the salon. Now Elaine is caught. Ah, she has this salmon lamé. A stitch here, one there, and at the opportune time—"

Janey rose from the chair. "You mean I hadn't gained that much?"

"In one week? The gown is waiting the time. This morning is the time, with Mr. Larson present. Now Elaine has a reason for firing you without losing trade from the beauty farm."

Mr. Larson chose that moment to stop at the door of the dressing room. For a moment he seemed too paralyzed to move. Janey noted his face closely resembled the salmon of the gown over the dresser's arm; then he was gone.

My goodness, didn't he know a girl wearing that gown couldn't wear much under it? And weren't people silly? He'd seen her in a swim suit twice as revealing. "Must be the lace," she decided.

Lola wheeled in, looked, grabbed a robe and threw it around Janey. "You'll take your death," she said breathlessly. "Now how long will it take you to pack? We have to leave right away."

"Are we going some place?" Janey asked with interest.

"My dear child, don't you realize you no longer have a position here? And you do have one at the farm?"

"Did," corrected Janey. "I can't support Grandma on thirty a week without hands."

"We know that. Hands knit in four weeks or so. We're giving you the J cabin. As I told Nick, I don't know of anyone more in need of a chaperone than you. The cabin is too awkwardly arranged for any but an employee, and with free room and board for Grandma—"

"Oh," said Janey.

For the first time since she had met Janey, Lola liked her. Imagine any girl being given free board, room and salary within walking distance of Nick Larson and not jumping at it. Maybe she was in-

69

terested in that funny-looking fellow in the horn-rimmed glasses.

"Better snap it up, Janey," advised the dresser. "Keeping two on one unemployment check's not easy."

Janey nodded.

"Thank you, Lola," she said gratefully. "Jimmy will, too, when he returns. Grandma's what's keeping us from getting married."

"She is?" Lola's beautiful eyes widened. "You mean she doesn't approve of him?"

"So thoroughly she won't let him support her until her annuities mature two years from next week."

"Oh," murmured Lola dubiously; then, "Oh." When she said "Oh" the third time in still a different tone, the dresser raised her head to look at Janey, opened her mouth, then closed it firmly. She'd already said too much for one day.

She could ask questions, however. As soon as Lola had issued crisp orders detailing where Janey was to meet the station wagon (Nick had taken no chances; it was in a public parking lot) and what they would accomplish on each step of the ensuing journey, she left.

"Janey, this beauty bit—how can it be farmed?"

"Cultivated," corrected Janey absently.

"You must have something to start with to cultivate. Me, I have nothing. And now," she pleaded

70

shoulders over the ruined frock, "I will not have the job to keep the nothing alive."

Janey, clothed now, straightened, listened and in another moment had grabbed torn and slashed material and scissors.

She wasn't a moment too soon. Elaine swept in. But before she could gather her fury, Janey was before her pointing to tiny darts, to fresh seams. She didn't have to say a word. Elaine grabbed the mutilated gown and sailed out.

"Now you have your job," said Janey, "and as soon as I learn beauty cultivation I'll have you out for a weekend."

"Imagine having something to look forward to."

For the first time since Janey had known her, the dresser's little face was illumined.

Loftily, chin in the air, Janey chose the main entrance for her exit. For a moment she stood outside remembering the dismal night of her previous discharge. Only three weeks ago? It seemed eons.

Two hours later Janey and all of her worldly goods went sailing out of the city in the back of the beauty farm station wagon. Nick and Lola occupied the front. Nick had said the front seat sat three, but Lola had pointed out it would be advisable for Janey to sit where she could keep two precious table lamps from crashing.

Janey didn't care. She was happy. She hadn't known being fired could be so much fun.

Nick, risking a glance in the rear view mirror,

frowned. "Janey, what are you worrying about?" he chided.

"Not worrying," she mourned. She was like a puppet putting on a beautiful dance, knowing someone else was manipulating the strings. Oh, well, Jimmy would be home in another week to do her worrying for her.

Meanwhile she enjoyed the ride, and when they turned onto the beauty farm road felt a warm sense of homecoming such as she hadn't experienced since childhood. Even cabin X looked possible.

Cabin X was what they called their "overflow." The four-armed dwelling appeared large from the outside, but each arm held its quota of double-tiered bunks.

For a girl who'd spent the past two years making down a bed divan each night, the largeness was a little overpowering. However, it did solve the overnight guest problem. With the exception of Elaine, everyone who knew her destination had suggested she might "drop in for an evening or so."

Trying to unpack her immediate needs before the dinner call, Janey considered the lure of beauty. Everybody wanted it in some guise: personal beauty, the beauty of jewels, of surroundings, possessions.

And some, she realized, went to fantastic lengths to gain it.

The buzzer caught her unprepared, and she went tearing up the broad path to the dining room, curls streaming straight out behind. She was a little late and made an entrance, and all heads turned. Jaded appetites picked up.

"What's a looker like that doing here?" grumbled a newcomer. "And what's she got to look so happy about?"

Janey sat at the high table and felt like an Oxford Don. She was above the restrictions laid upon all of those undergraduated eaters below.

"Well, Janey," Dr. Campbell beamed on her, "how do you feel?"

"Starved," beamed Janey. "I didn't eat any lunch because I was afraid it would show, but now that I'm fired—"

"An extra pat of butter on that steak," ordered Dr. Campbell.

At first the staff was fondly amused at her appetite, then concerned and finally alarmed.

"Girl, where do you put it?" begged Betsy Brown, the dietician.

"Oh, I'm well dug out," murmured Janey.

"Once," murmured Dr. Campbell, "a stray cat came out of the timber to join my family. She'd wail for food when she couldn't push another bite past her whiskers. But later, after she'd learned she could have all she wanted at any time, she became as choosy as my other pets."

Lola flared to Janey's defense. "If you are calling Janey a stray cat—"

"Heaven forbid."

Janey supplied the explanation. "Food and clothes and things. When I started to work at Elaine's I simply could not buy enough clothes. Later, after I realized I could have all I wanted at any time, she had to browbeat me to keep me up to the current style."

She caught Dr. Campbell's deeply probing glance and winced. Hadn't he said her love for Jimmy was caused by a can't-have complex? Once the barriers to their marriage were removed, she might find she didn't want him.

Fortunately she was distracted from dwelling on this. There were several offers to help in preparing her quarters. "It's easier to locate things if I myself have lost them," she refused, graciously.

Sally Stearns, freed of her Monoxide Gas title by courtesy of working in the office, stopped at Cabin X en route to her own, her dinner having been served by tray.

Wecomes over, she found a chair out of the direct line of traffic and in no time had Janey giving a hilarious account of her "final firing" from Elaine's.

"Must be quite a load off your conscience," observed Sally when she'd finished.

"*My* conscience," cried Janey. "Why, Elaine planned it that way."

"She thought she had no other choice. You clung to the job like a limpet. You didn't like the job or Elaine. Your attitude must have shown through the loveliest gowns you modeled. Stop sputtering."

Janey's sputtering died off rather than stopped.

Sally Stearns stood up. "You'll feel much better when you can bring yourself to write Elaine a nice note. Nothing like leaving the mental house clean. Gives you peace of mind."

It was one thing to concede privately she'd been primarily at fault, but imagine having to admit it in black and white.

Sally had suggested Janey put herself in Elaine's position and view herself from there. It took doing. She swung to the other extreme. Elaine was a harassed businesswoman with every employee and all of the trade against her. And she, Janey, was a miserable little gadfly buzzing around.

Some time after midnight the needle of her thought swung back to normal, but she didn't sleep until the note was written.

"Thank you for trying to let me resign from a position you knew I didn't like or want. I'm sorry I forced you to discharge me. As I am responsible for the salmon lamé being ruined, will you please bill me? I'll pay for it as I can."

Next morning Janey stepped into a world which seemed to have been turned over to diamond cutters during the dark hours. Every tree shrub and even the eaves of buildings wore festoons of shining white that blazed red and blue and gold in the sunshine.

A clean beauty, thought Janey. She felt clean too, somehow; cleansed of so much she couldn't name. Dr. Campbell could have labeled each: *frustrations* that had grown mildew; tiny drops of *bitterness* rapidly forming pools; a great block of *resentment*.

This was Sunday. Except for hostess duties she would have nothing to do. After breakfast the guests would congregate in the tiny chapel in the woods and there discuss some book of religious psychotherapy.

A wonderful day, thought Janey as the hours progressed. Each brought her closer to the one that would see Jimmy driving through the big arch. Between greeting visitors, alerting the guests to their callers and answering telephones, Janey spent the time inventing imaginary conversations between herself and one James Rainey.

"You look better already," Nick Larson remarked, turning back from a party he was conducting over the farm.

"It's this dress," she confided. "Any girl who can wear light coral should, at intervals."

"Not all the time?" he teased.

"Why do you suppose flowers change with the seasons?" she challenged. "They wouldn't be nearly as lovely if they were always there, wearing the same shade petals."

"Hm," buzzed Nick, then took a woman's prerogative: he had the last word. "But I was speaking of something shining out of your eyes."

Janey took those eyes to a mirror after he left. Contentment? Anticipation? Release of tensions? Or just the thought of Jimmy about ready for his return trip? Whatever it was it was good.

I know, she mused. It's like laughter.

Janey thought a lot about laughter in the next two days. As it was the first of the month, guests checked in and checked out.

The guests coming in were a glum-looking lot. Some scowled; some hadn't enough life in them to crease a wrinkle.

As if they had burned out light bulbs inside, she analyzed.

And those being released as cured seemed to have had new, super-watt bulbs installed and blazing.

She must learn more about the therapy which brought about this change. However, she never had time.

Any spare moment she spent on Cabin X. Someone had maneuvered a change in Grandma's itinerary. She was to be brought to a convalescent home not too far from the farm. From there to Cabin X would be only a short trip.

Janey stood in the center of the octagonal room

and tried to visualize it from Grandma's viewpoint. It was a wheel of inset windows and doors: windows looking out on views, doors upon tiers of bunk beds. A dizzy room.

She might sacrifice hope chest drapes and circle off one side of the cabin, but when she did she cut off the view of the kitchen terrace. The activity there might be a boon to a chair-bound Grandma.

To cut off the other view meant sacrificing a glade where a dogwood in full blossom vied with a stand of wild currant, rosy coral against young green timber.

Exasperated, Janey complained to Sally Stearns when she came calling. "I could almost believe Lola wished this on me to keep me from ever feeling at home."

"Whether she did or didn't isn't important. Accept it as an asset."

"This? How?"

"I don't know, Janey, but the principle works. It's like being given something you don't want, don't like. You can rail about it and keep yourself upset. Or you can accept the gift as part of some overall plan. When you do you find some delightful, unexpected use to put it to."

Anything delightful about sixteen beds when only two were needed would have to be unexpected. Janey grumbled, but she stopped railing and found that hanging drapes over doors left the view and created a sense of coziness. And at least she had room to store her things.

Fortunately she had everything in order by evening, because the next morning she became an active part of the beauty farm. She trotted the tanbark with heavyweights; she walked the woods with people whose eyes and minds were too clouded to see the beauty around them. In her spare time she attended to the work for which she had been hired.

She awakened with the birds but she didn't go to sleep with them. Instead she typed the next day's menus.

Sometimes she lifted her head to look around, usually at meal time, and realized she had never been busier or happier and surely never as well fed. She supposed she should pull her scales out from under one bunk where they had been pushed and weigh herself.

Saturday morning a quick glance in the mirror told her she must do something about her hair. It looked ragged.

When the morning mail brought a package from Elaine's and she found it contained a gray striped culotte with blouses to match every stripe and sandals to match each blouse, she blessed Elaine and her note which read: "Have fun in these, wise child."

Tomorrow Jimmy would arrive and find her looking nicer than he'd ever seen her. He might even think she was growing beautiful on the beauty farm.

Jimmy arrived instead that afternoon, just as Janey had trotted a current charge to the steam room and collapsed outside.

"Janey," Jim Rainey's voice held shock and distress, "what are they doing to you out here? You look like a picked chicken, all bones."

Chapter Seven

The incandescent light, which had been burning more brightly each day Janey spent at the beauty farm, went out.

"You don't look so hot yourself, young man," stated a voice, and Dr. Campbell came into view.

"Lack of exercise." Nick, coming up looking like Adonis and Hercules, rippled his muscles at Jimmy. "No oxygen."

"Deep-rooted resentment," mused Campbell.

"Improper diet," Nick too was thoughtful. "Well, we can take care of that. Now how long—"

"I," flared James Rainey, "am not an—"

He stopped. Lola had finally located her lodestar and was heading toward him, protectiveness in every step.

Janey looked at Jimmy, who was looking at Lola, and her heart dropped another two feet. Lola looked beautiful, as always.

What made the contrast between them more striking was that Janey was wearing a duplicate of Lola's "working workout" suit; in fact, it was Lola's. And as Lola was larger all around, Janey's appearance suffered the more by contrast.

"You must be Jimmy!" said Lola before Janey had a chance to introduce him.

"He—" blurted Nick.

"He?" asked Campbell in an unbelieving voice. Only Lola showed proper appreciation, and Jimmy liked it.

"I'll show him around," said Lola heartily. "You run along Janey, and get ready. What's his diet?"

"The works," replied Janey sadly.

"Then he'll be our guest." And off went Lola, her arm hooked in Jim Rainey's.

"I," stated Nick, "shall personally escort you to the dining hall."

"I doubt it," murmured Campbell. "Come on, Janey; to the beauty shop. Sally's getting her mop mowed, but she'll give her time to you."

"Janey," stated Nick firmly, "is beautiful as she is right now."

"I know it. You know it. Janey doesn't. She needs to." And grasping Janey's elbow, Campbell propelled her away.

Nothing, thought Janey, was more destructive to her morale than a trip to a beauty shop. First the wet dog look; then the skinned onion; then the girl from outer space with the rollers sticking up all over her head.

Janey ran the gamut of despair as she went through that hour. Lola, looking vital and beautiful, was taking her Jimmy out to view the very scene Janey had spent hours planning to show him.

Sally Stearns, primed by Dr. Campbell, just happened by Cabin X as Janey came from the beauty shop. Adroitly she led Janey to the proper clothes; not the new ones sent by Elaine.

"You'll probably go walking. Imagine red knees in the cool of the evening."

Later she said, "Never compete; be the best of your kind if you want to win."

Janey nodded. But she wasn't competing with Lola. That is, Lola wasn't competing with her. Lola didn't want Jimmy. And that was what made the situation so heartbreaking. It left her fighting thin air.

Lola rather overdid her tour of duty. She was late getting Jimmy back to the camp proper; however, they couldn't have arrived at a better time.

Word had spread! Janey, in a fluffy blouse, pleated skirt and bulky sweater, curls lifting in the evening breeze, was being escorted to the dining hall by pratically ever single man on the place. In the hall she was seated between Nick Larson and Dr. Campbell, just far enough away from Jimmy to keep him wondering at the laughter across the table.

Hm, thought Dr. Campbell, as succulent food normally enjoyed by Janey lay untouched.

Janey thought the time of torture would never end. Here Jimmy had been at the farm for three hours and, aside from his greeting, hadn't spoken a word to her. Nor had she spoken directly to him.

Sally took care of that. Chaperonage of even the best intentioned wasn't comparable to a few moments alone together.

"Latch onto Lola," she warned Nick, as she saw the physical director bear down on Jimmy making his way to Janey. That taking care of two of them, she hooked her arm in that of Dr. Campbell and led him away from the reunion.

Janey maneuvered him onto a side path screened from the general parade of bushes. "You look different."

"I had a shower," murmured Janey, unwilling to confess the lengths to which she'd gone to achieve the difference.

"Oh," said Jimmy, "of course. Here I write advertising copy on the best shampoo in the business —you know; 'Put a lilt in your looks.' "

She knew. Everyone within miles of her had samples Jimmy had given her because she refused to use the goop on her own hair.

"But you have lost weight," he charged.

"I wouldn't know. Dr. Campbell set up a routine for me, free of inhibitions. With me, scales are an inhibition. But let's talk about you. First, where did Lola take you on the tour?"

"We did every building on the place, even the kitchen. She's quite a saleswoman."

Janey nodded and promptly steered him west

by north, then turned him around. Sunset was busy splashing color on everything in sight, including Mt. Hood, which reared up wearing a cloud cap at a jaunty angle.

Janey was beginning to feel jaunty herself. If Lola seemed like a saleswoman to Jimmy, she needn't worry. He saw that type daily in his business, had for years, but dated only herself.

They came to a particular log Janey had long ago spotted as an ideal resting place, then sat a moment staring into space as though that might help over a time that had somehow grown difficult.

"Tell me about your trip," Janey said, finally.

"Oh, that. Sort of a refresher course. Deep psychology of advertising."

"Deep?"

"Depth," he corrected himself. "American public is getting wised up. The light jingle, the surface sales pitch is laughed off. We've got to get down under, reach that tender spot, understand?"

"No," said Janey promptly.

"Okay, take a coffee ad. We've been telling the public how it smells, how it tastes, how many more grains there are in the can of a given brand. Surface stuff. It doesn't relate—"

"Relate?" Janey sounded baffled. "Do it in words of one syllable, Jimmy."

"So we think deep. We think of the emotional value of coffee. We picture a chap coming home from work, tied up in tension knots. We build a fire on a hearth, put in an easy chair. He stretches out, feet to the flame, and reaches for a cup of steaming coffee. You see, you feel, you smell this symbol of relaxation in a spot of safe security."

"In other words you're not selling coffee; you're selling relaxation."

"No. If the viewer associates himself with the depth meaning of the beverage, he'll have an emotional response to our brand name every time he hears it, understand?"

Solemnly Janey nodded. " 'Lo the poor housewife,' " she murmured. "Picture her trotting around a supermarket trying to get a pound of chair, hearth fire and husband into a wire basket."

Jimmy ran long sensitive fingers through black hair. "No, Janey, you're trying to put the material side into the basket. Now tell me, what does this beauty farm mean to you?"

"Being myself," she said promptly.

"Being yourself? Haven't you always been?"

"Nu-uh, never. I don't remember my parents. Grandpa began making me into his idea of a little lady. Then grade school teachers took up where he left off. In high school and college there was an awful lot of concentration on turning me into a scholar. Then came Elaine and the girls and—"

"And me," stated Jimmy soberly, stood up and said they'd better be getting back. There was some kind of a gab fest at the lounge. Lola had told him he'd understand Janey better if he attended. She'd be there, wouldn't she?

Janey, who'd had every intention of walking her Jimmy into the lounge, promptly changed her mind.

Soberly they walked back, Mt. Hood not doing a thing for them. He reared up like an ancient man, mist cap pulled down over humped shoulders. He looked the way Janey felt: gray, defeated.

Jimmy left her at the administration building looking more owlish by the moment. He'd be seeing her after the meeting. Janey doubted it. There'd be music and dancing and refreshments. She couldn't see Lola letting go until the last guest had been tucked in.

"Hmmm," buzzed Sally as Janey entered, "not going to the lounge? Good subject tonight; might help you with your immediate problem."

"I doubt it. I wouldn't hear a word. Sally, you go for me."

"I've been," Sally returned.

"Then tell me, what is there about it that will help Jimmy understand me? Lola told him it would."

"She did?" Sally's face brightened. "That's good news. In laymen's language, the general idea is to teach those present how to know themselves, analyze their reactions, learn how to respond for or against. It means Lola knows the rift in your romance lies in Jimmy's subconscious; she's not out to pick him off for herself."

"I know that; what worries me is the way she's wrecking the romance before the rift is located. Jimmy didn't once mention our plans. And he didn't ask about Grandma."

"Want to tell me the subject he did discuss?"

"How to sell coffee," muttered Janey. "Sally, how does one learn to know oneself? Is there any short cut I could take?"

"Honey child, you never left it, really. You're like a weighted toy. You let others push you off balance, but once they remove the pressure you're back on center again."

Janey nodded. She'd had such a toy. And what a time the poor thing had had getting back on center. It would go round and round, rock, bump and finally come to a stop only to go through the same gyrations at the next push.

"Guess I'd better learn to redistribute the weight so I can't be knocked around in the first place."

She took a scratch pad to Cabin X and settled down, her back deliberately toward the lighted windows of the lounge.

First she would review this last happy week. Why had it been such a gay, lilting stretch of hours? She'd told Jimmy it was because she'd been herself. What had herself been?

She had never worked so hard. Ah, but no one

had asked anything of her, except menus. She'd seen things that needed doing and had done them for the fun of it. She'd gone out with new, difficult guests who'd grudgingly accepted her company on their first field trip, then had asked for her after that. Why?

Maybe because I let them alone, she reasoned. I went along and had a good time for myself.

Now how was that going to help her with Jimmy? He'd come out to the farm to see her the moment he arrived back on the coast. Then Lola had stepped in, and he'd like that. And he'd considered going to the lounge, at Lola's request, more important than spending the evening with his fiancée.

It was at this point she swung around and looked at the lounge. Guests were dancing. On impulse Janey sped out to stand close enough to watch couples pass the big window.

She returned slowly. Jimmy was having a wonderful time. He'd seemed so animated she'd gone clear up to press her nose against a small pane. He was dancing with a grey-haired woman, a new guest; his head was tossed back, his beautiful teeth white with laughter.

I guess he needs to be left alone by me, she reasoned morosely.

Could it possibly mean that he'd be as happy being fired from her heart as she'd been on being fired from the salon?

"I'll give him back his ring," she murmured, then realized she couldn't because he hadn't given her one in the first place. She'd suggested he put the money in their house-savings account.

Then how was she going to let him know she was firing him? She might make a play for Nick, but she'd be likely to lose her job if she did, and there was Grandma to consider. Dr. Campbell's wife wouldn't like her making up to him, and there wasn't a male guest on the farm just now that posed a threat.

For the first time since she'd been at the beauty farm, Janey used the mental trash box, a gadget that was an integral part of every bedroom on the place.

Carefully she wrote down her problem, tucked it into the box, then, knowing it would be there in the morning if she needed it, turned out the light and went to sleep.

In the morning she lighted a match and burned it where it lay. The idea had seemed silly, but it worked. She now had an answer she wouldn't have had had she turned and tossed all night.

The birds were barely awake when she slipped a note under Sally's door, then scurried along a woods trail that provided shelter clear to the bus stop.

The health and beauty farm went into quite a tizzy that morning. Janey was late for breakfast, and Janey was never late where food was concerned. Sunday morning breakfasts were special, with food designed for leisurely enjoyment.

Nick sent Lola down to the X cabin, and Lola came back, eyes bugging. Janey wasn't there, and her bed was made. Had she gone walking in the woods the night before and become lost? Met a bear, a cougar or an escapee from something more than natural wilds?

Jimmy, feeling wonderful for the first time in six weeks, arrived at the dining hall in time to catch the full impact of the alarm.

Janey was missing and presumed lost!

Methodically he discounted dangers. Cougars rarely attacked humans. He doubted if the bears around the farm would harm her, provided she saw them first. He'd taught her how to conduct herself in the wilds.

"Then maybe," Lola held a hand to her mouth to press back a scream, "she walked into a pit and has lain there all night with a broken leg!"

The hue and cry was on.

Sally was the last to hear of it. She still wasn't able to work up any enthusiasm over breakfast and had arranged for coffee and toast on a tray to be brought to the office.

Unfortunately she had made a roundabout trip to her cabin when the first bulletins were went out from the switchboard.

Forest rangers on foot, in jeep and by helicopter joined the search.

Hastily gathered photographs of Janey were flashed on television screens as bulletins. Radio programs were interrupted to blare forth the disappearance of the beauty from the beauty farm.

Miles away, Janey heard about some beauty being lost. Thrilled at watching a mounted posse get ready for a take-off, she asked if there was to be a parade.

Gravely the nearest leaned from the saddle to shake his head. "Beautiful woman lost in the mountains," he intoned.

"She'll be all right if she doesn't lose her head," Janey comforted him, then saw the crosscountry bus pull in and hurried to catch it. Grandma wasn't supposed to have visitors in the morning, but she'd pleaded an emergency. She thought they'd let her into the rest home.

Chapter Eight

Let her in? She couldn't get through the crowd on the veranda.

There was Grandma McBride striding up and down.

And the radio was blaring so loud Janey could hear it from the roadside and all the way up the drive.

"Beauty Lost On Beauty Farm," came in staccato barks from the announcer.

"Grandma." said Janey.

"Hush," said Grandma. "Maybe they've found the child. Imagine the poor little tyke lying out all night with her leg broken."

"Maybe dead," offered a well wisher.

"Who's died of a broken leg?" Janey persisted.

"You have," stated Grandma McBride, wailing.

"Oh," said Janey, and sat down, because dozens of elderly people were gathering around Grandma with handkerchiefs.

Sally had made connections shortly before this. She'd tried to help at the switchboard but had been brushed rudely away by Nick. So she took her Sunday newspaper and went back to her cabin.

But Sally came equipped with what was known to her friends as a "ten-thirty hunger." At ten-thirty she sought the kitchen to poke around for something to ease the pain.

"Isn't it awful about Janey?" mourned the cook. "They're sure she's dead. She'd never go without breakfast this long."

"She probably stopped at the café when she changed busses. She left here on the six-thirty; the place should have been open—" Then: "What?" screamed Sally.

Janey sat on the veranda wishing people would quit milling around. She was tired. She'd worn her model-tread slippers, and while they gave her that certain something on the avenue, they gave her something else on country roads.

"Bulletin. We interrupt this program—"

Vaguely Janey listened. What was a beauty doing on a beauty farm anyhow? Couldn't be the health and beauty farm, because there were no beauties there except Lola and as far as she knew Lola never got out of sight of Nick.

Suddenly the radio was snapped off. A dead silence reigned. Janey looked up. Eyes, dozens of them, were staring at her accusingly.

"How could you do this to me?" demanded Grandma McBride.

"You might have pretended at least. The shame of such a let-down!" snapped another.

"Pretended?"

"Remained in the woods," said an authoritative old man, "made yourself look injured, acted exhausted. Young woman, do you know how many men have been looking for you all night? Hundreds!"

"But I haven't been lost," Janey complained. "I slept in my own bed and walked to the six-thirty bus and came straight here, so how could I look injured in the woods on a bus? You've been listening to that news bulletin and mixed me up with it."

"Janey," Grandma was beginning to bubble, "you are *it*."

"I am?" She thought of the posse setting out, riding right away from her after talking to her; of the people she'd seen at the bus depot as she had had breakfast.

No wonder no one had recognized her. They were looking for a lost beauty, and she had been neither lost nor a beauty.

Grandma, who'd sunk into a chair, had been pried out and now conducted Janey to her room.

"Now explain this early visit. You must have started at dawn. Up to your old tricks, aren't you? Not wanting to make trouble for anyone, you didn't wait for someone to drive you in; you just—"

And then she burst into laughter. Janey hadn't wanted to trouble anyone.

"And how is dear Jimmy?" asked Grandma.

"Dear Jimmy," announced a brittle voice from the doorway, "is ready to turn Janey over his knee. Will you, *can* you tell me why you took off without letting me know?"

"In the first place," Janey explained patiently, "I didn't know where to find you. In the second you'd been at the farm eight hours before I went to bed, and within that time you'd shown no personal interest in me or my plans."

"And just why did I go to that fool winging at the lounge if not for you?"

Grandma McBride looked at her hands. She couldn't lever herself out of the chair without help. She could rock herself out, but the one time she'd tried that she had landed smack on her face, this time protecting her hands. Oh, well, she might as well enjoy this. "Why?" she added to Jimmy's query.

"Because you fell for surface advertising," Janey informed him.

Jimmy suddenly became aware of Grandma. "What happened to you?" he demanded.

"I went roller-skating," she replied pleasantly, "on one skate."

"At your age?"

"The older we are the flatter we fall. Jimmy,

why don't you take the girl out and feed her? Remember she's been lost in the woods."

"Grandma, I *haven't!*"

"Something tells me it's going to be too bad you weren't. I don't think the beauty farm is going to like the publicity you've given them."

Dramatically Janey turned. "Then I'll go get lost."

"Hadn't better," warned Jimmy. "You can't cry wolf twice. This time they'd let you lie."

"Of course," mused Mrs. McBride, "a good public relations man could twist this into a fine promotion campaign for the farm. Might even work up an advertising contract on the strength of it. Alertness, care of guests, that sort of thing, with little asides on how the farm cultivates beauty."

"And bouquets tossed to Forestry and the posse; coverage by radio and television. This being Sunday morning, the newspapers didn't get in on it. You might have something there. I'll get onto it. Come, Janey?"

"I just *et,*" she stated flatly.

Jimmy got clear to the driveway before that penetrated, whereupon he loped back in. "Come get in that car or I won't be able to map out this campaign. If I don't you won't have a job. Now get going."

"My," breathed Mrs. McBride, "if your grandfather had ever spoken to me in that masterful tone I'd have swooned at his feet."

Janey had never felt less like swooning, but she was stopped from expressing herself by one word: job. She could not bear being fired from the one place she was allowed to be herself.

On second thought, she'd been herself that morning, and what had happened?

"Get the lead out," Jimmy ordered gruffly.

On the other hand, she'd done nothing. She'd left word. She'd had the day off. She had taken the day off. Now how would Dr. Campbell explain the result?

Dr. Campbell, Nick Larson, Sally Stearns and all the rest of them—none of them ordered her around. Each of them made her feel beautiful. Maybe that was the magic of the beauty farm: being made to feel what one wasn't.

"I had hoped to talk to Grandma," she said stiffly, "seven rooms worth."

Jimmy gave Grandma a pained look, but she seemed to be as addled as her granddaughter. "I spent another week's worth," she replied. "Maybe you can return after Jimmy has your job nailed down."

Jimmy insisted that would be an all-day job, and Grandma McBride nodded. "Just as well. Half the home town is coming to visit me this afternoon. Janey, in that desk is a thick envelope. One of the guests here is a former private secre-

98

tary. She has listed the disposition of my worldly goods according to my desires."

Jimmy tiptoed all the way to the car, ushered Janey in as thought he expected her to crumple, then, on his own side, turned a worried countenance on her.

"You should have told me yesterday. How long?"

"How long what?" asked Janey, studying the thickness of the envelope.

"Has Grandma got?"

"Another week," she replied absently.

"And you can sit there and take it like that? Think only of her worldly goods? Janey, what has that beauty farm done to you?"

"I don't know," cried Janey, exasperated, "but I hope and pray you'll find time to spend a few weeks there. Jimmy, you need it. Grandma's going to love it."

Patiently she explained that Grandma had another week at the convalescent home, then would move to Cabin X for an indefinite stay, at no cost.

"And that?" He pointed a long finger at the papers Janey had taken from the envelope to read.

"A list of what she wants to keep; the rest is to be sold at auction, after we've weeded out anything we'd like to have."

Dr. Campbell might have explained Jim's sudden upsurge of spirits. An early meadow lark trilled happily in the field across from the home, and Jimmy wanted to trill with it. He didn't know why. Eventually Dr. Campbell would explain dim nightmares in which he'd tried to fit Grandma's golden oak and Mission atrocities into the modern home of his dreams. Grandma without her furniture was much more digestible.

For the next two hours Jimmy Rainey poured charm and salesmanship over the city. He made promises. He recalled past favors.

Radio and television began talking about and showing a beauty farm where care of guests was all-important.

By evening, when Jimmy telephoned the beauty farm, after waiting half an hour to get through, a weary Sally reported Nick Larson was not available. A board meeting was in progress. The farm had had so many calls for reservations they were drawing up expansion plans, a new building program.

"Tell Janey to come home. All is forgiven," she concluded; "even Lola for triggering the panic button."

Jimmy nodded at the telephone. Here he'd been blaming Janey, yet when he stopped to analyze it had been Lola who'd sold them on the idea of Janey "lying dead of a broken leg."

"Yet if she hadn't," he reported to Janey, "we wouldn't have had this sympathy for the farm as a blast-off."

Janey nodded. She supposed he was making

sense. She was too tired, too disheartened to care.

They had driven to Grandman's home town, unlocked the door of the deserted cottage, walked through, tiptoed out and locked the door. Then they'd unlocked it and returned.

"And to think I've cursed the age of plastics," muttered Jimmy. "Imagine owning stuff that refuses to wear out, especially when it looks like this."

There wasn't much they could do in the limited time allotted them. Grandma's clothes and personal effects, photographs, treasures, all the car would carry were loaded. They'd return as soon as Janey and Jim could find time off.

Jimmy knew an auctioneer. Janey knew a woman who'd come in to clean once the house was empty. Jimmy said he supposed he should bring Grandma out for a final pick-up before the auctioneer arrived, and Janey said Dr. Campbell had warned her against it.

When they drove into the farm it looked as though a spring festival were in progress. Every light was on, though it was not yet dark outside. Cars packed the parking area. People walked the paths. The administration building looked like a beehive with figures coming and going.

"Nice timing," said Jimmy with satisfaction. "People with nothing to do this early in the year heard the story and came out to view."

"Hm," said Janey.

The car was spotted immediately. Nick Larson loped up, beamed at Janey and spoke to Jim. "Fellow, we need you. Come on into the board room. Janey, Sally's ready to drop; can you take over?"

She could. She went into the office looking so bemused the weary Sally laughed. "You catalyst," she charged.

"But I didn't plan it that way," Janey protested. "Honestly, Sally, I haven't had a minute with Jimmy. Oh, we've been alone together, but one or the other of us was always off some place, if you know what I mean."

"Speaking of being off some place, so am I. The farm needs my cabin and I don't. This morning's experience cured me of not eating breakfast at the proper time."

No, she didn't know where she was going; she never did. To know would be like reading the last of a book first. But she'd keep in touch with Janey.

Janey watched her drive off the next morning. It seemed to her she was always watching people drive off. Jimmy had barely pecked at her cheek, then had shot out to his car and driven off the night before. He'd had to catch Stedman.

Dr. Campbell came to the office after a last word with Sally Stearns. Her cabin was being made ready for the next guest.

"We're seating her with you, Janey," he said. "Thought we'd better brief you."

"You mean I'm back on all protein?"

"No, you can both have the same as our table. This woman isn't eating at all. In fact," he looked at her sternly, "she's an attempted suicide case. She tried to take the wrong exit to get away from a domineering mother. Her mouth and throat were badly burned in the attempt. She's been discharged from the hospital as cured physically. We want to give her a reason for living."

Janey was worried. "But what do you want me to do?" she asked.

"Just be yourself. I only told you this much to prevent you from saying something that might be misconstrued."

"Then I'm not to psychologize her into eating or—"

"Janey, Jim Rainey told me what you liked about the farm was being allowed to be yourself. People are like plants: left alone, they can usually straighten up. This," he glanced at a card, "Stella Louise Shelly has been crushed down by a strong personality. Psychological props would come from the outside. She'd depend upon them. If she's left alone, her strength will develop from the inside. Right?"

"Of course," agreed Janey in a thoughtful tone, then went trotting back to the office.

A car had driven in in her absence. A young, rather saucy-looking girl stood in the doorway. "I'll say you need someone here to look after this place. I'm Meg Moran, the new reception clerk.

Where's Larson, the fellow I talked to on the phone this morning?"

Janey had seen the axe hanging over her head at Elaine's. Here she hadn't had the faintest suspicion they had one. Yet here she was, replaced without notice.

Nick came in, moving with his usual swift quietness. "You must be Miss Moran," he greeted the newcomer. "You've met Miss McBride. Janey will you show Miss Moran your duties? I doubt she'll find them too difficult."

He glanced at his desk then, said, "Oh," and from it took an envelope, "I supposed this had been handed you; Lola said she'd take care of it."

Janey accepted the envelope, swallowed, longed to run for cover before opening it, then bravely took a letter opener and slit the flap.

Chapter Nine

A moment later, just as she had collapsed into a chair on her arrival at the farm, she was sitting again, this time staring at a badly typed page.

"I don't think I understand," she murmured.

"Ah then, we'll have Miss Moran go to her room to tidy up while we discuss it. Right?" he asked. "I'm sure you won't mind her using one wing of the X Cabin overnight. Good; I'll be right back."

Janey put in the longest ten minutes of her life as she waited. She read, then reread the note, and thought it was no wonder Lola hadn't been anxious for her to receive it.

I, she informed herself, am sort of an ambassador without portfolio. I don't have to do anything but be myself. By name I am hostess, a member of the staff proper. And I start at fifty a week, with board and room for both myself and Grandma.

She would also relieve the Moran girl as Sally had relieved her.

That, Nick explained when he returned, was what had started the idea into fruition.

"Sally pointed out how often we were calling on

her to relieve you because we needed you for some guest.

"With this boom in business, we know you'd be called more and more often. We found you were typing nights to keep up with your work. We wanted you free for more important work. So we created a position."

Janey shook her head. "I still don't understand. What am I supposed to do?"

"What did you do to Henshaw?"

"Oh, that." She thought of the irascible man who had exhausted every male member of the staff as he went on his self-imposed hill-climbing punishment. Finally Janey had been elected to accompany him. The first day she had come in winded, the second only slightly out of breath. On the fourth day they had ambled in, arguing.

"He tried to tell me a white-crowned sparrow was a white-throated one. We got into a terrific argument, and I told him he never slowed down enough to identify anything correctly, that I'd prove him wrong, so he slowed down."

"And then—"

"I couldn't be with him all the time, and he decided to sketch the birds with their identifying marks. But they wouldn't sit still long enough, so I suggested he take color photographs. That's all."

"He gained five pounds, a decent disposition and a hobby. You see, Janey, his wife was an invalid and amused herself with such bird watching

106

as she could do from a garden window. His only interest was in keeping feeders and fountains near that window. When she died he transferred his resentment of her passing to birds. He thought he hated them.

"He's a man who has to have an avid interest in something. Some place along the line you made some remark. Now he's embarked on a save-the-birds campaign."

"Oh? Goodness, if I'd known—"

"Janey, had you known you couldn't have done a thing for him. People are sick, mentally and physically, because others, oftimes inferiors, try to help them. We can give mental and physical therapy, but we can't put in that spark that makes them find life worth living. That has to come from within, touched off, we're finding, by a disinterested person busy being herself. Just keep it that way."

Nick left, leaving a tender smile for Janey to consider.

It was all too deep for her; she'd just sit and be thankful for the new job and the raise in pay. If this good luck kept on, she could save enough to buy Grandma a small cottage and stop worrying about paying rent. Then she and Jimmy could seriously consider a split-level and—she stopped there.

This was one job she couldn't hold while married to Jim Rainey. And what happened to Miss Moran?

Janey finally all but tiptoed down to Cabin X. Inside, she could hear low, broken sobs, far apart. She nodded. She'd had those herself. Miss Moran was in the tapering off stage. She'd begin making a noise and give her a chance to clear up the effects of the deluge.

She succeeded quite well. She kept on tiptoeing and crashed into a stack of cartons they'd brought from Grandma's house the night before. Miss Moran appeared at the inner doorway.

"Jackpot," said Janey solemnly.

"Breakables?"

"Probably. I'm good at those."

"You too?" The voice rose in a wail.

Janey grabbed a handful of paper handkerchiefs and thrust them at Miss Moran without looking at her. "Great to wash things out of your system, isn't it? Nice thing about this cabin, nobody can hear you. Bathrooms over there when you want to clean off the efffects; it's about time for the luncheon bell."

"I can't eat. Oh, I'm hungry enough, but I just can't take anything that doesn't belong to me. And this job doesn't, because I lied to get it. I," she spoke slowly now, "was fired from my last job and the one before and the one before that."

"That puts you two up on me. But then I only had one to be fired from."

"And they hired you here anyway?"

"Right in the middle of being fired."

The memory struck Janey as so ludicrous she had to tell about it. Before she was through Meg Moran was laughing in a hiccoughing fashion.

"But my firing was different. I talk back. I'm flip and sassy, and if I'm mad enough I tell the truth."

"I was inclined to indulge in that luxury myself."

"You don't understand. I can tell that wonderful Mr. Larson the truth. He might give me a chance, but I couldn't promise I wouldn't sound off at some guest."

"You won't. When you know it doesn't make any difference whether you do or don't, you don't."

Meg mouthed over this gem of wisdom, bewildered, and Janey tried to explain. "When my weight was vital to my job, I could gain on an ounce of lemon juice and thought of nothing but food. Now that it doesn't matter, I eat what I want and don't gain. But neither do I want the rich food I used to think I'd die if I didn't get."

She let it go at that and scurried off for a tray, sending Meg to the office after facial repairs.

En route she met Dr. Campbell and, intent upon establishing Meg's defense in advance, sought to tell him about the girl.

"Oh, we know all about that," he said easily.

"Her former employer found out through some staff member we'd hired her. He felt it his duty, he said, to warn us."

Janey went on, then hurried back on the run. "Dr. Campbell, suppose Meg really talks up to a sensitive guest, what then?"

Out of his pocket Campbell took a small box with a slit on top. The face of the box showed a head like Meg's, a twisted mouth from which came the words: "Oh, yeah? Well, let me tell you—"

"Miss Moran will have pad and pencil beside this. Right from the beginning she will write what she wants to say. The following morning she will empty the box reviewing her blow-ups of the previous day. She'll find them pretty silly."

"Oh," said Janey and went back on the run for Meg's tray.

Returning at the sedate pace the tray demanded, she did quite a lot of thinking. She'd been right in what she'd told Meg. This mad box was merely designed to protect the guests, and of course alert Meg to her habit.

She stumbled, felt someone move smoothly to her side and relieve her of the tray. "Now what has cast a cloud over you, Janey?" asked Nick Larson.

By the time Lola reached them Nick had gone into his reason for wanting to talk to her. He'd like her to go to the cabin prepared for Miss Stella

Shelly and see if she could discover anything that might be added for her convenience or comfort.

"Here," she handed him the one extra dish she had removed from the tray for safety, "you feed Meg. I'd like to be away before Miss Shelly comes in."

"Remember," Lola tossed after her, "the guest has never been away from her mother, except at the hospital, for a single night. She is twenty-five."

Janey remembered. She even slackened her pace at the thought of it, then set off at a real run. She had work to do.

One look inside the best cabin on the farm and she was off again, this time to find Dr. Campbell.

"I didn't know whether I was in a florist's shop or a funeral parlor," she protested. "There are cut flowers and potted plants, and every one of them smells sickly sweet. I read one card. Couldn't help it; it hung right out with big letters. It said, 'Never forget mummy loves her little girl.' Gosh!"

Campbell chuckled. "Her physician has ordered Mummy to stay away from her until she's called by her daughter. You run on to the library. I'll have everything moved to the hothouse where she can see them if she wants to. We can hand her the cards with her mail."

Janey sped on to the lounge, almost deserted now that the lunch buzzer was about to sound.

For a moment she stood very still. Suppose, she

had found life so little worth living she'd tried a painful escape, what would interest her?

Nothing, she admitted dolefully.

She tried to picture herself as a crushed plant, but her stem kept sticking straight up, waving a blossom on top. And that blossom was curiosity. Now what would spark this Stella's curiosity. A factual story of someone in her age bracket starting life over again.

Janey found two: one of a woman of forty, with whom this Stella could identify; another about one eighty. That would prove one was never too old. She chose a few others, enough to fill a small tabletop shelf, and scurried back to the choice cabin.

"Now then," Janey put herself back into Stella's shoes, "if I had trouble swallowing, I'd hate like the dickens to eat before people. But if I had snacks in my room I could nibble, start the eating habit."

Janey had lunch in the kitchen, walking around, assembling tempting non-perishables for the choice cabin.

Dr. Kathryn, passing through, made audible protest. "You know we don't encourage food in the cabins, Janey. We want our guests to have the right food at the right time."

"Umhum, but if you had the habit of rebellion, wouldn't you rather sneak a few bites than have your innards revolt at having to eat what was put before you at a given time?"

"We could send trays."

"Oh, but that would be almost the same. The guest would be sure you'd check the trays on their return; she'd still be eating under supervision. This way she could start being herself without pressure. And once she knows there will be none, then she'll come up to the dining hall, starved."

Not only did Dr. Kathryn agree; she went to her cabin, returning with a guilty expression, an electric plate, several small cans of soup and a can opener.

"It's worth the experiment," she conceded.

Janey had a wonderful time. This was like Cabin 7, only more so. It was "having a place of one's own."

Carefully she pulled drapes back from a window looking out on a sharp rise, draped now in a wild bleeding heart, the delicate pink racemes a dainty contrast to Canada mayflowers shooting white stocks through the feathery foliage.

The quiet, secluded spot of beauty should give Stella a sense of security.

Janey checked the set of small books on local flowers and birds, on stars and mammals, then impulsively reached for one she had brought from the library. In a moment she was sitting on the floor, Stella, the cabin, everything forgotten.

The sharp buzz of the bell brought her flying to

the administration building, the forgotten book face down on the cabin floor.

"Get a load of that," Meg Moran demanded in an awed tone as she entered.

That was a car such as Janey had rarely seen, and driving it a stiff-visaged chauffeur, now getting out to open the door for the woman beside him.

The woman stepped out, chin at an arrogant angle. She scanned the health and beauty farm, and one could sense her disgust. Then she shrugged her shoulders.

"What's the matter kid? You look kinda sick."

Janey felt "kinda sick." She'd thought the cabin so beautiful, so comfortable, so desirable. But for a woman like this? The cabin shrank in size and desirability, and when Janey thought of the snacks she'd provided, she shuddered.

"Up and at 'em," Meg urged her. "Larson's legging it this way, but you're elected to take her to her digs."

Janey let Nick Larson reach the car first. Nick, she thought, could reduce even this gal to some semblance of humanity.

I'm to be myself, she reminded herself. What's myself?

Perversely she thought of Elaine, and of Sally telling her to see the real Elaine as a harassed business woman rather than as a dictatorial employer. Now she must see this Stella person not as

114

an obviously wealthy person on a slumming expedition, but as one who'd tried to flee from life because life wasn't worth-while.

She was trying so hard, at the time Nick introduced her, she made an indelible impression. She looked so completely preoccupied Stella Shelly waited only until the chauffeur had deposited her bags and departed to ask a question.

"Are you in love with that man?" the voice came in a husky croak.

Janey's lashes flew up, "Oh, I hope not," she murmured. "Grandma and I need my job, and Jimmy wouldn't like it at all. He's my fiancée," she explained.

"I see. Now if you'll call the maid—"

"We don't have maid service." Janey drew a deep breath. "Maids intrude. They only come in to do the cabin when you ring for them; otherwise you do exactly as you please when you please."

"Ha. Nobody does that."

"I know. That's what I thought when I came, but—"

"You mean employees—"

"I didn't come as an employee, but they didn't know it until I'd started to work. Mr. Larson had me mixed up with a girl he'd hired by telephone. I guess I thought work was part of the therapy."

For the first time a faint spark touched the completely expressionless face.

Janey moved around, indicating features of the

cabin, the snack closet. "I can bring in anything you'd like."

She stumbled over the book she'd left on the floor, blushed and admitted she'd been "sneaking a few pages of reading when her call came."

"Love story, I suppose?"

"Oh no, it's factual."

"And love isn't?"

Hmm, thought Janey, there is more than a domineering mother in this.

"The only rule we have here," Janey drew a deep breath, "is that guests must not go on long hikes alone. It's too easy to become lost."

"Like that silly model who wandered off Sunday." Stella walked away from the garden window to look out on the camp.

Suddenly she wheeled on Janey. "That man out there, the one getting out of that car, who is he? I must meet him."

Janey peered out. That was Jim Rainey. To think of all the quiet plans she had made to interest Stella in living, and then to have her pick on Jim! What should she do? Admit he was her fiancée or be true to the beauty farm?

Now she studied Stella. Despite her immediate past, Stella was pleasingly plump; a compensation eater. A few weeks at the beauty farm and she'd be Jimmy's ideal.

Chapter Ten

Walking to the administration building, Janey reviewed what she had said, even as her glance swept the immediate vicinity for some sign of Jimmy.

She had told Miss Shelly the man was Mr. Rainey. Asked if he worked at the farm, she had said no; he was with the Joe Stedman Advertising Agency. When the new guest demanded to know if he would be dining at the farm, Janey could only say she had no idea, whereupon she was ordered to find out.

Janey arrived in the office to find Jimmy's blue eyes emitting sparks, Meg madly writing on her scratch pad.

"I asked a civil question," Jim greeted her, "and does she answer? No, she started scribbling."

"Civil!" burst from Meg. "Janey, he asked me what business I had taking over your job and who was I anyhow. Want to see what I answered?"

"Tomorrow." Janey found she could laugh a little. "I've been promoted, Jimmy. And, Meg, I made the same mistake this morning when you came in."

Jimmy smiled and Meg gave an impish grin. "So you're the wonderful Jimmy."

"Today," he qualified, and added, "thanks to Grandma McBride. Either of you girls know where I'll find Nick? Have some copy I want him to okay."

"Jimmy," Janey forced the question between teeth that wanted to set, "are you staying for dinner?"

He glanced at his wrist watch, said, "Why not?" then caught sight of Nick and loped off.

"Janey," Meg asked after a few minutes, "what's wrong?"

"Oh, I'm just trying to be myself. All of a sudden it isn't easy. Going for a walk," Janey murmured, and started out.

Meg called something, but Janey neither heard nor cared to hear. Head down, brown eyes watching the tips of her walking shoes, she ploughed on, hands deep in her sweater pockets.

Here she was on the first day of her new job, a wonderful job in this wonderful place, and she had a problem too big to handle.

Now why, after meeting Nick, was Stella Shelly interested in Jim Rainey?

She was vaguely remembering the Shelly name now. Money in capital letters. Hadn't Elaine once fished for their patronage, then sighed and asked who would compete with Paris?

Suddenly a named popped into Janey's mind:

"Shilly-Shally Shelly." That was what someone had called Stella. Now she remembered. Two girls had been gossiping. One had said nothing would come of an affair with some man. It was she who'd invented the Shilly-Shally, and the other had reproved her. "Mama won't let her be anything else," she'd said. "Mama will settle for nothing less than a big name."

Maybe now Mama would. Maybe Mama would buy Jim.

"Janey!" Janey jumped, then found she herself had snapped out the name.

"Janey?" a voice called. "Oh, there you are." Jim Rainey came around a bend in the path. "Janey, have you lost the little sense you had?"

"No," she replied absently, "I've just found a good supply. Did you want something, Jim?"

"Meg said she told you to take a raincoat, but here you sit, soaked."

"I'll dry."

"Well, come on. Janey, does it occur to you we never have a moment alone any more?"

When she merely stared, he shrugged. "Oh, I know we were together all day yesterday, but we had problems riding with us. And the day before—"

"We had little Lola," Janey agreed. "Was there something special you wanted to talk about?"

"Right now I want to get you out of this rain. Look, instead of having dinner here, why don't we run over to Zigzag? Then we can talk without someone popping off in our ear every moment."

Janey nodded. "Jim, do you know a Stella Shelly?"

"Stella Shelly?" he mused, then brightened. "Sure. At least I've met her. Think it was three years ago, time I played in the tournament at Waverly. Ed and I came in off the course, and she was waiting for him."

"She checked in today. While I was with her she saw you, asked who you were, then wanted to know if you'd be dining here."

"She did?" How dared he look so pleased? "What's she doing here? She used to be a knock-out."

"Maybe she's trying to retain what she has."

"Well, I can see her another time. How about Zigzag?"

Janey lost what ground she had gained that evening at the rustic inn, with rain slanting on the outside of the windows, firelight reflecting on the inside and Jim gay and eager.

He'd won the beauty farm account. He was working up a fall promotion campaign. He'd had some rather good ideas, and old Joe Stedman was thumping him on the back so hard he'd have to see an osteopath.

"Couple more accounts and we won't have to wait. We'll buy a house big enough for the three of us. How does that sound?"

"Wonderful," breathed Janey, all of the little bristly nerves lying down peacefully. "Jim I'm so tired of being shuttled around."

"Probably's what's keeping you thinned down. How about the Shelly girl? Somebody told me she really put it on; was as portly as her mother."

"She's what you'd call perfect," Janey admitted honestly.

"Who's she engaged to now? Seems she's great for making and breaking engagements. Heard the boys in the locker room talking one day after she'd given Ed the brushoff."

"Why would she?"

Jim smiled. "No money, no prospects; just a good guy with a lovable disposition."

Janey wanted to relay the conversation she had overheard in the salon but couldn't. She said merely, "She wasn't wearing a ring."

"Not getting any younger," Jim said sagely. Then he switched the subject abruptly. He'd talked to Nick and Stedman. They, he and Janey, would be free all day Friday. He'd pick up Grandma, then call for her, and they'd all drive to Grandma's cottage.

Later they'd bring her back to the farm.

Janey got out of the car at the arch so Jim wouldn't be held up by a chance meeting with anyone. And she wouldn't have to explain to Miss Shelly why Janey had walked off with the man she wanted to see.

121

Swiftly Janey hurried up the driveway, rain hood pulled over her brow. Ahead lay the half-circle of lights, the great blaze where the lounge windows fanned out cheer on the wet spring evening.

She'd hurry to her cabin, Janey thought, take out the memories of the evening, polish them to go with the horde of other evenings; her security against days of doubt.

But first she would check with Meg.

Meg Moran was writing furiously when Janey stepped in. One look and she crumpled the sheet. "Thank goodness you're here. Please get over to that Shelly dame, before I blow my top. Honestly, she's kept the wire hot asking for things and service we don't have here—and for you. And is she ever arrogant!"

Janey waited only a moment, then asked Meg to locate Nick. A few words with him and she had her answer.

Miss Shelly came to the door immediately. "Of all the lax, inefficient, indifferently run—"

Eventually she ran out of adjectives. It was then Janey asked evenly, "Would you like me to call your home and have your chaffeur come for you? We like our guests to be comfortable; if they're happier elsewhere we do nothing to keep them here."

There came another rush of words, but behind them Janey sensed fear. Made brave by this, she said, "Why don't we sit down and talk this out? Most guests have a rugged time the first evening. I didn't, because I was too tired, and had a real bed after two years of sleeping on a makedown divan—"

She said she had fallen on her face. And she talk about the apartment, and having to sit up on a kitchen stool when the other girls had dates, and how wonderful it had seemed to her to have a place of her own where nobody would intrude.

"There is that," murmured Stella Shelly.

"And a chance to be myself," Janey went on. "It seemed to me my friends were all pulling or pushing in different directions, and trying to get along with them—"

She worked as she talked. She'd seen the tray with the untouched food and felt guilty. Now everything on it was shriveled or wilted or dried. But there was the snack shelf she'd fixed up. She could make cream soup with chicken cut into it poured over toast to soften the crispness. Later she'd run to the kitchen for an ice.

"And now," the arrogance was leaving, "are you, as you say, being yourself?"

"I'm improving, but it takes time. I had to stop and weigh the cost even though I know no cost is too high in the long run."

Miss Shelly, eating hurriedly and swallowing painfully, paused. "How do you mean that?"

"Well," Janey curled up in an easy chair behind

123

the guest, "it's this way. When you try to be what another demands, you're not yourself. You begin being filled with resentment at being somebody else. And finally you blow up. Then both of you are hurt—the one who has tried to make you over, and you yourself because you've finally found out."

"Go on," urged Miss Shelly.

The words came painfully, "I guess you finally find out that they didn't like you as you were in the first place or they wouldn't have wanted to make you over."

And then because she didn't want Stella Shelly to see the tears stining her eyes, she jumped up. "I'm dashing over the the kitchen; be right back."

A weary Janey entered Cabin X an hour later. Meg lay on the divan asleep, exhausted as Janey had been her first day at the farm.

For a moment she stood looking down at the little monkey face and thought she knew Meg's problem. Life wouldn't be easy for one wearing a face everyone poked fun at. For a girl of spirit, fists would always be doubled to strike in defense. What could the beauty farm do for her?

And Stella Shelly could have been beautiful yet somehow wasn't. There was no light about Stella. She was more like a porcelain statue.

Janey went in to make up Meg's bed, laughing at herself. That morning she'd wondered how she could possibly fill her time just being herself.

By careful steering, some unsnapping and the rescue of one slipper from between the sheets, Janey put Meg to bed.

When she had time to think of herself and the painful conclusion she had reached in the Shelly cabin, she was too tired.

On awakening the next morning, Janey had every intention of being unhappy. She had reason to be. Jimmy might love her but he didn't like her. Imagine spending a whole lifetime with a man who would be forever criticizing her. Why, in no time she'd be back at the farm as a paying guest, trying to unkink.

I feel miserable, she told herself on arising.

But Meg seemed to feel more miserable than she, and in her effort to cheer the other girl her own normal spirits began creeping up. Besides, on such a morning it was difficult to hold them down.

The sun, its face well washed the previous day, flashed golden light all over the landscape. Flowers tossed the night's raindrops from their heads and glowed in what television insisted was living color. As for the air, a few deep breaths and Janey felt intoxicated and also starved. She was the first to answer the breakfast call.

The older members of the staff watched in envious admiration as she enjoyed every bite of her breakfast and some of theirs.

Dr. Kathryn shook her head. "Janey, I had wanted you to take on Mr. Davis today. He's so eager to lose weight he's liable to kill himself in the effort. I thought you might take him strolling on easier paths."

"Two-ton Tony?" asked Janey, with a final blissful sigh. "Why not? I wasted away for a month when his touchdown won the state championship. I thought I was in love with him."

"Good, you'll speak his language. A little admiration might turn the fat into muscle, but slowly."

"He still is impelled on that terrific drive," Dr. Campbell explained.

"So we divert the drive?" asked Janey. "How?"

That was the problem upon which they were working. Maybe he'd let down the barrier talking to her.

Janey wasn't sure. He'd been a mighty senior when she was a lowly freshman, and because he hadn't been too studious, giving his all to athletics, had been even older than most in his class.

Oh, well, all she had to do was be herself.

She found that quite difficult. Herself could not keep up with the young mountain who, having reached a decision to take off weight, was going after it, head down.

"For Pete's sake, Tony," Janey sprawled over a log hidden by sword fern, "Call your signals when you spot such interference. To think I ever rah-rahed a bulldozer."

Anthony Davis came to a rocking stop. Aside

from a snide, "They didn't even send a boy; they sent a girl," he'd paid no attention to her.

Now he blurted, "You know me? You couldn't. You're just a little tyke."

"I'm five foot six, and let's not go into weight. I had to come out here to lose some."

"You certainly succeeded. How'd you do it?"

They found a fallen log and perched on it, unaware of bird song, of an azalea that had beaten the season by thirty days to blush cream and amber in its sheltered spot.

"I lost it the hard way the first time; then I gained most of it back. Then I came out here and didn't care, and off it came. You know something, Tony? I'm beginning to wonder if we don't gain because we eat what we're told not to, so we eat more to cover up the guilty feeling."

"Do that over," he urged.

"Well," she sighed deeply, "my fiancé likes girls that look like pen-fed partridges. So after I'd been fired for being overweight, I was hired here, board included. I thought I had it made. I could eat all I wanted, gain weight and Jimmy's favor."

"And what happened?"

"I hit my normal weight and stayed there," sighed Janey.

"You look okay to me. Look fit. What's the matter with that fiancé of yours anyhow?"

All of the blue shadows in the woods pooled to saturate Janey's spirit. Wistfully she told the big man her deductions, and he commiserated with her.

"I'm in the same boat but not in the same way," he confessed. Then out it came, the whole unhappy story.

He'd married right after leaving college and had gone into professional football. His wife had, she thought, married a hero, a shining light on the field. Then the overweight and his ticker started acting up. He'd had to find an easy job, and right away the love light in his wife's eyes dimmed. She, he whispered, began seeing other men, fellows on the professional teams.

That had upset him so his heart had started doing somersaults, and here he was, a broken old man at thirty.

Morosely Janey nodded. The wife, she reasoned, hadn't loved Two-ton in the beginning; she'd loved the limelight. Now how could she tell him he wouldn't suffer? Wives were different from fiancés.

"Any ideas?" Tony asked.

"Umhum," she agreed slowly. "You love your wife, right? Well, when she fell in love with you, you were the limelight. Maybe, finding that light dimming she figures you're not making the most of your potentials."

"Look, Janey, I can't go back into—"

"For goodness sake, Tony, there are other things than football. Maybe your wife has matured faster than you and thinks that's adolescent. Maybe she's trying to push you into some other kind of limelight, the kind you throw off when you're sure you're making the most of yourself. Now what do you really like to do?"

"That's out of the qeustion; it would take a year's training."

"Your wife went back to her profession because she was bored, you say. Okay. Maybe she'd be happy enough to work this out with you. It's worth a try, isn't it?"

"I gotta think that out," he said, and from then on said not a word during their long, easy stroll.

That was unfortunate. It gave Janey time to think her problem out. It was most confusing, but she had the answer. And she was going to stick to it.

Chapter Eleven

Janey would have felt worse had she had the time. Reaching the farm proper, she found Meg signaling from the administration building.

"It's that Shelly dame, but I've done all right. Only wrote one remark at her."

"That is an achievement. Hope I can do as well. What does she want?"

"Just you, period."

"Half an hour. Oh, Meg, you go to Dolly at one-thirty for hair styling."

Now what had she said? Janey's mind flashed back to her own lean days. "No cost here, you know; just the farms' idea of keeping their employees up to their advertisements."

"Yeah, but you don't know how long it took me to grow this haystack hair-do."

Janey walked on to the Shelly cabin, her mind swinging back and forth between Meg's hair and her own problem like a huge pendulum, though what relation there could be between the two she didn't know.

"Unless," she whispered, "Meg and I put a lot

of uncomfortable effort into conforming to something that wasn't for us."

Once she glanced up to find the nearest hills looking like pincushions, with the dark blue of fir and hemlock so many pins stuck into pale green velvet. Deciduous trees were leafing out; spring was catching up with the calendar.

If she once had time to go out by herself and think—

She hadn't. Blinds were drawn at the Shelly cabin, and when she entered at a command, she found Stella in bed, the room in complete disorder.

"You've got to get me out of this miserable place," Stella told her. "I rang for breakfast and was refused."

She ranted on until Janey longed for Meg's vocabulary. She wanted to say, "Oh, stow it." Instead she waited for the other to run down, then asked. "Why did you come here?"

"To be alone."

Slowly Janey shook her head. "Your side of being alone is having a lot of people around you can boss."

The Shelly face turned a delicate lavender. Never had she heard such insolence. Patiently Janey waited.

Finally, tired of the silence that followed, Stella asked irritably, "Aren't you going to say anything?"

Janey nodded. "I think so. I think you're big enough to take it." She looked through to the next room, which showed evidence of Miss Shelly's attempt to prepare a breakfast of sorts. She hadn't even known how to use a can opener.

"You say you came here to be alone. That means you're seeking personal freedom from something, and that's good. But it's something you have to earn. Everything has its price. Part of the price of freedom is loneliness."

Eventually she threw out the challenge: "It's easier to lie in bed and have people wait on you than to walk up the mountain, but lying in bed can be awfully dull. You've found that out. It's going to take more strength of character to get up and start using your muscles than most girls with your background have. I wonder if you have it?"

They had lunch together at the dining hall. Miss Shelly made an entrance and was shocked to find not a head turned in her direction.

"Isn't anyone interested in anybody but himself?" she asked when they were seated.

"I'm not; are you?" Janey flashed. "You, for instance, were thinking not of the people but of their reaction to seeing you here, weren't you?"

Later she explained that most of the guests were new. After they'd been at the farm a week or so they'd be looking outward rather than inward. Then she wondered when she was going to start changing her own view.

At the moment her whole attention was focused on Friday when, with Jimmy and Grandma, she would drive up to close the only real home she had ever known.

She was glad Friday turned out so beautiful, the mountains standing out like pasteboard cut-outs. It would make things easier on Grandma. Personally, she'd have preferred a deluge of rain to match her spirits.

By the time Jimmy and Grandma drove in both were in a gay mood. And of course they were late in departing because Grandma thought she had to see everything. She even raved about Cabin X.

Of course Jimmy would think of Grandma's hands and have a lunch prepared so she could be hand-fed in the privacy of the car. Now how was a girl going to fall out of love with a man like that?

And he would choose a turn-out on top of a mountain so they could look down on thousands of acres of hilltop and valley, all sun-drenched, all stirring with spring growth.

He would also say irritably, "You're not eating. I don't know why you think you have to keep that slat figure at the beauty farm. Here; now take this drumstick."

"How can the girl eat with you yapping at her?" Grandma asked equably.

Janey, who wanted the chicken, found she couldn't have swallowed it had it been ground to liquid and poured down her throat.

133

"It's all right, Grandma," she said absently. "Quickest way to be fired is to—" Her voice died away, principally because both began talking at once. They hadn't understood she meant Jimmy wanted to be discharged from her heart; they were thinking of her position at the beauty farm.

"Janey," Grandma's voice broke her reverie, "what are you thinking—about whom?"

"Two-ton Tony," she murmured.

She was. She was also very quiet the rest of the drive, because she was thinking of the advice she'd given Tony: to find something which would create an inner limelight to make up for the outer one he'd lost.

When Jimmy had first met her she'd been a glamorous model, and even though he'd not approved her figure he had, she believed, secretly enjoyed the limelight, though not admitting it to himself.

So she'd seek a career. What? The only talent she seemed to possess was being herself. At the moment that wasn't helping her much. It kept her busy, but it wasn't doing a thing for her relationship with Jimmy.

When the car went down into the valley, Janey felt it was going down into her past and her grandmother's for below lay childhood memories.

She needn't have worried about Grandma becoming depressed at having to leave; she even seemed glad to be through the chore of telling

Jimmy which article to mark for the auctioneer, what she "supposed she should keep."

"Don't you even want this coffee table Grandpa made?" asked Janey, shocked.

"No, it could burn up in ten minutes, but the memory of Hal working on it I can carry with me always."

When, late in the afternoon, she walked calmly out without a backward glance, Janey felt a little shocked until she remembered something Sally had told her. She had learned to "travel light." She had finally given up some family antiques because it was easier to carry them in her mind than to polish them every Saturday morning.

Jimmy too was quiet, slightly disapproving, and Janey wondered if he was thinking of the aunt who revered tradition. Jimmy had been reared in it by the aunt, whom Janey had never met, because she rarely left her home in the southern part of the state and they hadn't found time to visit.

Janey stopped in the office while Jimmy drove on to the X Cabin to unload Grandma and such spoils as she'd thought worth bringing.

"Have they been giving you a bad time?" Nick asked when Janey came in.

She shook her head. "I don't know what's wrong, Nick."

"Promise me something?"

He was leaning on the counter, looking down at

her, his blue eyes wise and tender. What could she say but yes?

"Stop blaming yourself and stop trying to make yourself over to someone else's pattern. We like you as you are. Ask Campbell," he concluded.

Janey hurried on, after promising to return and take over to free him for dinner, and felt completely revived. It was wonderful that someone saw you as practically perfect, even if you knew you weren't.

Meg, having a rest hour, was having a ball with Grandma, Janey found. She also found a new Meg. The short haircut intensified the gamin look, seemed to make Meg look authentic.

"Why isn't Lola sitting in for you?" Janey asked.

"Didn't you hear? Sickness at home. She's taking her vacation early to give them a hand. Your Jimmy is driving her in to the plane."

"Well, that was fast," was Janey's only comment.

Meg scurried off to the dining room, and Grandma McBride turned a parental eye upon Janey.

"Are you in love, or do you think you're in love with that Greek god running this place?"

"Why?" demanded Janey.

"Jimmy snapped at you for a hundred and fifty miles, and with every snap you sank lower and lower. Then five minutes with that Mr. Larson, and you look water and aspirin."

Solemnly Janey nodded. "Maybe it's because he doesn't snap. He's kind and makes me feel as though I had a normal supply of brains with maybe just a few extra."

"Hm. Is Jimmy in love with this Lola person?"

Janey had to smile a little. "For his sake, I hope not. Lola thinks Nick is Adam and no men have been created since."

"You don't mind Jimmy driving her to the airport?"

"Lola? Nu-uh."

"Hm," said Grandma.

Dr. Campbell had quite a talk with Grandma McBride that evening. He came down to the X Cabin while Janey was saying goodbye to Lola and Jimmy.

It was strange, Janey thought, turning back to the office, but she didn't mind Jimmy going off with Lola, even though he'd merely pecked at her cheek and said, "See you Sunday, maybe."

Lola had been quite upset over something. She'd whispered a subtle warning to Janey: "You will keep your eye on Miss Shelly, won't you? She's really in no shape to see other members of the staff just yet."

Later, talking to Stella, Janey had to explain her absence that day and why she would not have so much time in the future. Grandma's hands were knitting, but she still hadn't free use of them.

"But why bring her to a beauty farm?" cried Stella. "What does a woman her age want with beauty?"

Thoughtfully Janey answered, "If this farm grew potatoes, just being a potato wouldn't do anything for anyone would it? They would have to be distributed, used. Maybe beauty's like that: something to give out to others."

Stella's laugh wasn't pleasant. "And you think if Grandma can be made beautiful she'll be an inspiration to everyone who looks at her."

"I didn't mean that at all. I'm beginning to see beauty isn't just face and figure and a good appetite. Stella, I'm not good at words, but put it this way. I doubt the sun is beautiful to look at, but it certainly makes one feel good when it shines after a long winter. It brings out beauty in everything it touches."

Stella said she needed her head examined, and Janey would have agreed, but Stella went on talking.

"Now take Larson. He's like the sun. He beams on all his paying guests. And he is one beautiful man. But not for me. I'd rather have that thin black-haired man who drove in the other day. I'm sure I've met him some place."

"You have," sighed Janey. "At the Waverly Country Club. He played in a golf tournament there three or four years ago. Ed somebody introduced you."

Stella grasped Janey's wrists and shook them. "I must see him again. Promise me you'll bring him here or arrange for us to meet the next time he comes out."

Wearily Janey agreed. The meeting was inevitable.

"What," demanded Dr. Campbell the next evening, "have you done to our Stella? She's developing a shine. She even went to Doctor Kathryn on her own power and asked for the best our medico had to give. She told her she wanted to become radiant."

"Me and my big mouth," moaned Janey, and relayed her talk on her conception of beauty.

"Not bad, not bad at all. But, Janey, you might start applying this yourself; you're looking just a little droopy. Not carrying too big a burden with Grandma, are you?"

"Oh, no, she's fun. It will be all right. Just give me a few days. I'm trying to practice what I preach, and it's not easy. I'm forming a new habit to replace an old one," she explained.

The old habit drove in the next day. Sunday dinner was just over, guests and their visitors streaming from the dining hall. Stella, busy practising beaming, didn't see him at first.

Jimmy, told where to find Janey, came striding toward them, and Stella was ready.

139

"Introduce us; then scat," ordered the regal one.

Janey performed the introduction. She turned blindly away and ran smack into Nick Larson who, for some insane reason, put his arm about her and walked her off.

Janey looked back once. Jimmy didn't even know she had left.

"That man-eating shark," Nick grumbled.

"Don't blame her," Janey defended her. "This started long ago."

"Don't you mind. Wait till the season's over. I—that is, we'll make it up to you. You're doing fine work here, Janey."

Jimmy came in much later. Janey had seen Stella hook an arm in his and turn toward a particular walk Janey had been saving because the mock orange was coming into view and the little glade where the walk ended looked exactly like a chapel all dressed up for a wedding.

"And just what," Jimmy demanded of Janey, "happened to you? Stella and I looked around, and you weren't there."

Chapter Twelve

"Jimmy, it didn't matter one way or the other. You wanted to go with Stella. I had other things to do. But I have come to a decision. Being engaged is difficult for both of us. I am becoming un-engaged to you until I don't care whether I am or not."

They had a beautiful row. Dr. Campbell, a deliberate eavesdropper, had quite a time to keep from cheering.

"You," stated James Rainey, "have become a complete nitwit."

"Then you should be relieved. Imagine wanting to marry a nitwit."

"I had hoped they could do something for you out here. They've a record of some outstanding cures."

"You should try it some time."

"Me! Me? Why, I—"

"You are becoming so critical it's sheer misery to be in your company."

"It's Larson," stated Jimmy firmly.

She let him rant a little and finally silenced him. "Jimmy, it isn't anyone else."

"Then you don't love me."

"The funny thing is I do," she retorted. "It's just your attitude toward me I don't love. Oh, dear, let's forget reasons; just consider me unengaged to you."

"You're jealous, and you aren't big enough to let me tell you what Stella Shelly wanted of me."

"She told me in advance," sighed Janey.

"I'm going to see Grandma; maybe she can talk some sense into you."

However now that Grandma could lever herself out of a chair without landing on her knees, she was not becoming involved in any quarrels. Nor would she take sides.

"But, Grandma, do you know what this is going to mean to me in a business way? Old Joe is so sold on Janey he swears by her. Why, this could put our marriage off for years."

"Becoming unengaged could?" she asked innocently. "Jimmy, drive carefully going back. We don't want you out here as a recuperating casualty. Remember now."

Dr. Campbell, who knew his Sunday evening traffic on a resort freeway, used the red herring approach. The board was getting together right after supper; they wanted Jim to work on an idea they'd present. He'd be there, of course.

Fortunately, new guests had arrived, and Janey was so busy being herself all she felt about Jimmy was numbness.

There was the angry businessman who swore he was being railroaded to keep him away from a board meeting where his presence was vital to his own interests. His physician had told him if he attended, the interests would belong to his heirs; he wouldn't be around to care.

"You're certainly a bright spot," he grumbled at Janey. "I thought a hostess radiated cheer."

"Supposed to. It's like the time I had my appendix out," she explained. "It's numb now, but I know it's going to hurt tomorrow."

"What's like an appendectomy?" He looked around the cabin.

"Me learning to feel casual."

"About what?"

"Anything." Automatically she picked up the coat he'd flung at the bed and which had lit on the floor. "You see," she hung up the coat and turned back, "when the chips are really down your only chance for peace and happiness, which are one word, is not to care whether you do or don't. Then you won't."

"Do that over—that last bit."

"Do you swim?" She had checked his card and knew he did. "Or play golf? What happens when you use fury on a golf club or, while you're swimming, get mad and fight the water?"

Slowly the big head nodded. "Best score I ever made was the day I went out with the wife. No men to compete with; she's a rotten player, by the way. Then there was my long distance record in the Gulf of Mexico. I got fouled up in an undertow, started to fight it, then remembered and eased up. It carried me out fresh as when I started."

"Both times you didn't care and relaxed."

Janey walked around, moving a chair to a slant where it would catch the last glow of the sun on a far mountain top, pushing the books she'd chosen where an unwary hand just might fall on them.

"Yah!" He kicked a chair in turning. "Business is different. Drive, that's what it takes; a goal, then a fast, hard drive toward it."

"I wouldn't know," she commented. "I'd think that such a drive would be a dead giveaway to opponents. As with that golf game, if you didn't care, really didn't care, they'd get the message and wouldn't bother blocking the goal.

"Goodbye now; I'll try to smile at you tomorrow."

" 'Bye," he grunted, and sank into the chair.

Slowly Janey made her way up the hill to a cabin she particularly liked, a cabin which was gay and cheerful even at twilight.

The girl inside was anything but gay. With dull black hair, scaly skin, lusterless eyes, she sat humped over staring out on the mountains.

This was one place where Janey's theory wouldn't work. This Sharon Herbert did not care and was despondent. She seemed lifeless until

Janey entered; then there was a sudden look of panic.

"I'm sorry," she apologized after a moment. "I have this peculiar feeling at the strangest times."

"Stress," said Janey. "You had to work up extra energy to meet a stranger after you'd used up all you had coming to a new location. Does it feel as though you'd been wired from head to toe and all the wires were vibrating?"

"How did you know? And tell me why my boss sent me to a beauty farm of all places?"

This Sharon had been a brilliant young business woman, engaged to an attorney and looking forward to his political career. Then came a virus; one that recurred with not enough time for her resistance to be built up. And now she no longer cared.

"Your boss," Janey told her, "found out what was wrong with you; he wanted you back as you were. Now you're like a car in perfect trim, all gassed up, but with the spark missing."

"The spark? Oh, now, look. I've been on diets, taken bottles of vitamins—"

Janey remembered her card, the three words scrawled across it: "extreme biotin deficiency." The antibiotics used to destroy the virus had destroyed the good as well as the bad bacteria and, until they were replaced, neither food nor vitamins were of use.

"Don't think about it," Janey advised. "Just

look ahead three days. I promise you'll be surprised at how much better you feel. We're having a tray sent over."

"Please, I am not hungry, and I do not intend to be forced to eat. It only makes me ill."

Janey stood thoughtful for a moment, then nodded. "When you feel that way, do what a guest here did before she came here. She'd go into a market, gag, then think of the thousands in the world who were dying of hunger because there was no food available. She'd be so ashamed of her ingratitude for what she had, she'd buy, prepare and eat though she suffered for it.

"Only, as of now, you won't suffer. Try it. Even this first meal will go down and then lie cozy."

Janey waited for the tray, then stood by, asking what Sharon thought of the Attorney General's attempt to save the beauty of the coast's beaches by controlling right-of-ways to off-coast oil drilling. And Sharon found a faint sparkle, forgot she was eating and accepted two capsules without comment.

She left with the suggestion Sharon try a book beside the bed as she waited for sleep. It was a historical novel on the beaches in question and the way Indians had felt about them.

Walking back to the X Cabin, she decided the farm was a good place to experiment with her theory. Reviewing others' troubles minimized her own. Now if she could get through this first talk with Grandma, who'd probably rant and rave.

But Grandma didn't. Dr. Campbell had had the forethought to see to that. He'd called to find her sunk in gloom.

"If Janey hadn't had to help me they'd have been married," she explained.

"Well, thank your lucky stars they weren't. It's easier to become unengaged than unmarried."

Grandma said she loved Jimmy as she'd loved her own son. Campbell agreed he was a fine fellow, but as of now not the right husband for Janey. And there wasn't a thing he could do about it. Members of the board were selfish individually and collectively. Janey had a quality which reached the guests quicker and more effectively than any professional pronouncements any of them could make.

"She'll find her way," he promised. "Just leave her alone."

And then he switched her interest to her hands. If she didn't start using her fingers they'd stay splayed out like starfish prongs. He suggested picking up pins as a beginner; later, maybe painting. She might try their hobby classes and find something constructive to do with her spare time.

Janey reached the cabin, shoulders squared, defenses up.

"All right," she greeted her grandmother.

"Let's have it and get it over with. I know Jimmy came here; what did he say?"

Grandma yawned. "I didn't pay much attention."

"But, Grandma, we're unengaged."

"That is your business isn't it? What possible good could I do either one of you by taking sides?"

"I did think you'd tell me whether you felt I'd done right or wrong."

Mrs. McBride shook her head. "I wouldn't know. Each individual looks upon life through a different window, the frame of which is his accumulative characteristics. We may be looking at the same general view, a hillside or a valley, but what actually lies within immediate range of this vision is as individual as a thumb print."

"Thank you," murmured Janey. "That explains Jimmy and me. We were looking out on marriage but each seeing from our own window frame. Gram, does marriage widen the frames or maybe bring them together into one window?"

"Let's say it allows a couple to look through each other's windows steadily enough to become familiar with each other's view."

Janey started her immediate future feeling as though a weight had been cut out of her life; there was a sharp soreness. Nor did she find her usual zest in living—until a Mrs. Carol Johnson came in. The Johnson was an assumed name.

148

The board decided they should brief Janey more fully. They'd written on the Johnson card, "No will to live." But that wasn't enough; she should know what had brought this young matron to such a blank wall.

Janey could have read about it in any newspaper. Believing her husband away on a business trip, Mrs. Johnson had spent the night with a school friend not known to her husband's friends. The following morning she had opened the newspaper to find her husband's photograph on the front page with that of two others, his secretary and her husband. All three were dead.

"Neighbors of the secretary supplied the police and reporters with the unsavory details," Dr. Campbell told Janey. "They proved to be correct. Mrs. Johnson—or so we call her here—had no immediate family. Through shock and disillusionment she lost all will to live."

"Not another suicide attempt?"

"She didn't care enough to try."

"Just be yourself," they advised as she started on her chore.

Stella Shelly appeared before her, dressed for walking, "Oh, Janey, good news. That lamb Rainey telephoned this morning. We're having dinner at Zigzag on Thursday."

Zigzag, thought Janey, angrily. Why did he have to take her there of all places?

So she had taken a chance and lost. What kind

of a goal could she find now that would take the place of her dreams of being married to Jimmy?

"I'm sorry," Janey stammered. She had entered the cabin at Mrs. Johnson's weary call to come in, then had stood there, silent. "I just received an emotional upper cut that left me groggy. I'm awfully afraid I'm not going to be all sweetness and light."

The colorless lips of the woman twitched a little. "You'll be honest; that's refreshing. What are your particular duties here?"

"I'm supposed to be a hostess of sorts, kind of a tucker-inner. The other board members analyze and find out what's wrong with their guests, what needs correcting or curing. I—" She broke off. "Hey, I think I've got it. I find out what's right."

"Suppose there is nothing either wrong or right; just nothing?"

Janey sank into a chair without invitation. "I'd just say to move over; me too. Only—"

There was silence; then Janey began to think out loud. "Sally was a guest here. She'd had some fantastic blows. Sometimes she'd been ready to give up, but she couldn't. She'd been born with an outsized bump of curiosity. She just had to go on living to find out what was going to happen next, good or bad. She said they evened off pretty well if you had the gumption to see them through."

"And if you hadn't?"

"Then you pretended you had. She had to pretend she was hungry for three months before she woke up one day and found she was."

"Appetite!" scorned Carol Johnson.

"There are other things too—goals," she remembered, and arose to show Mrs. Johnson the call bells, the card indicating the hours meals were served, where to find books and magazines, and belatedly the hobby shop where handcraft was taught.

Not a flicker of interest crossed the woman's face.

"I'm sorry I've been such a flop," Janey said contritely, preparing to leave, "but *I* feel better. I remember now what Sally said about goals. When one gets knocked away by disaster, pick another one and head in that direction. That's what I have to do, and it won't be easy."

"Why bother?"

Janey considered this. "I don't like selfish people, and that's selfish. It spoils the other fellow's view; you know, like a raddled old stump in a lovely flower garden.

"Mrs. Johnson, I do hope you won't tell the board the way I've poured my troubles out on you."

The sardonic line of Carol Johnson's lips changed. The girl, Janey, was sincere. Being sincere, Janey had left her feeling like a "raddled old

151

stump." Maybe she could do something to help Janey.

Goals, thought Janey, heading toward the administration building. She needed a new one. What kind? Not romance; she wasn't ready to put anyone in Jimmy's place. Shouldn't she be thinking of a career, a hobby at least?

She would the moment she found time.

The angry man caught up with her before she'd reached the door. Could she accompany him on a stroll?

Since she had no choice, she did.

"How are you coming with your theory?" he asked when they were under way.

Janey looked up at him, her eyes shadowed with pain. "I'd no idea it would be so difficult," she confessed.

"I know. I decided to try it; just for fun, you understand, haven't made much progress." A fist knotted to pound the palm of the other hand. "I get so doggone mad when I think—"

"You do?" cried Janey. "I did this morning; then I talked to a guest and decided I needed a goal. If I can locate a new goal and keep my mind on it, my other problem won't seem important. Pretty soon it won't matter if I do or I don't."

"Any ideas?" The angry man looked less angry, more interested.

"Nu-uh, nothing seems too important. Have you? Maybe if you could think up one—"

The big man and the not so large girl stopped to stare at a low bank where fiddlenecks were trying to make up their mind about unfurling.

"Ha," said the man, "gives me an idea. I took in some worthless property on a deal. It's way up in the hills south of here. Might make good sheep land. Don't know a thing about sheep, but I'll bet I could learn."

"House on it?" asked Janey.

"Nope."

"Then I'll pretend a house for you. How big do you want it?"

Janey didn't know how the story got around, but it did. Of course they'd sent off for books on sheep on the hoof and in the raw; on grazing; on markets. And they'd ordered an assortment of government bulletins.

Building a house on paper carried Janey through Thursday evening. Not that it was easy. Jimmy drove in, looking like the original man in the grey flannel suit. He saw her, came up and kissed her, slapped her on the shoulder and said, "Be seeing you, honeychile." Then he went out to dinner with Stella.

That was bad enough. The next day Stella came to her, not looking too well or too happy. Janey went to the Shelly cabin, sat down and watched Stella pace. Then she wheeled.

"Janey, I need help. I want to plan the kind of a country home a man would like. Not a big one;

153

just one that a man on a small salary could manage without sacrifice to his pride."

At least, moaned Janey inwardly, it wasn't a split level.

Chapter Thirteen

Janey nodded as Stella talked. Jimmy had dreamed of the day they could afford a weekend home. He'd spoken of it as a cabin. Stella was describing a lodge.

And then Janey perked up. Jimmy couldn't bear to be indebted to anyone. If Stella built such a place as she was describing, a fisherman's paradise, Jimmy would be off her hook.

But would she want him back when he'd raced to Stella after becoming unengaged to her?

She'd better start being herself. Sighing deeply, Janey turned practical.

"How much do you want to spend?" she asked.

"Money's no object," Stella said airily, then turned to Janey, an expression of shock on her face. "Oh but it is. Janey, do you know something? I have no money."

"Oh, dear," said Janey, for there went her last defense against Stella.

Stella echoed the "oh dear" and sat down across from Janey.

"Janey I'm going to tell you something, and if you ever open your mouth—"

"I wish you wouldn't," objected Janey, for she might reveal something Jimmy would need to know, and Janey would suffer from split loyalty.

"I must. None of my own friends could possibly understand. They'd think me crazy. But you—well, you're used to being without money."

Janey then received a vivid word picture of Shelly's past. She had had every material thing a girl could want except money. And she knew why. Her father had quietly accumulated what her mother had released to him until he had enough to take off to parts unknown. Her mother had reported him lost on an African safari, but she and his nephews, who ran Shelly Incorporated, knew better.

Janey thought it better not to ask how her mother had gained control in the beginning and nodded.

"So she was afraid to let me have more than a few dollars at a time."

"Your beautiful car is worth quite a few."

"It's in her name, and I was never allowed to drive. Everything is in her name—well, almost, everything. I do have two hundred and fifty a month from Grandma Shelly, but what can I do with that?"

Janey knew she could have done quite a bit with it, but Stella was different.

"I guess you have to decide which is more important: freedom or roughing it. If you owned a

156

little place you might make it. I could, easily, and enjoy it, but your life has been so different."

Stella picked up one of the books Janey had left. "This woman managed on a lot less. And she enjoyed every minute. And this old lady in her eighties—why Janey, they lived. They did what they wanted to do; they didn't have someone standing over them ordering even what they should eat.

"Janey, this I promise. If I have to go back to that other way of living, I'll make a good job of it this time."

Janey shrugged. "Both of those women were brave enough to take life as it came; they'd never have thought of running out on it because they couldn't stand up and declare their own rights."

"You," stated Shelly, "have never met Mama. She doesn't work in the open. She builds traps. She manipulates behind the scenes. I've watched her work on others. You can't win, ever."

A ring flashed as she brought a hand flat down to emphasize the point and gave Janey an idea.

She spoke of her grandmother's refusal to advise and said she couldn't advise Stella. But if Janey were in the same position, she would begin gathering everything she did own, gifts and such that could be turned into money, and build up a freedom fund.

Surprisingly, Stella kissed her as she left.

"I have to go," Janey insisted. "Mrs. Johnson

wants to drive to her home to pick up some things she needs before it's put up for sale. I'm to go with her."

"Would she take me?"

Janey hesitated. She didn't know.

"Oh, I know all about her," Stella said. "Her picture was in the newspaper for days. But I wouldn't let her know I knew."

"I think that's up to her," Janey decided.

Talking to Mrs. Johnson, who, it seemed, had also heard of Stella, Janey felt miserable, yet the latest guest seemed a little less stone-like.

"I was once a lowly member of a charity committee her mother headed. If this Stella is like her mother, she's completely self-centered. If she isn't, she's desperate. We might as well give her a chance."

When Janey hesitated, Mrs. Johnson said, "It will make me feel less like a raddled old stump in a flower garden."

Janey was called on the carpet a week later. It had been quite a week. Jimmy came out often, each time greeted her affectionately, then took Stella out for dinner. And Nick, after the first time, managed to be within fast walking distance, tossing out such obvious compliments Jimmy's long face grew longer, the twist of his lips more sardonic.

Yet it was good to let him know a man like Nick thought her beautiful.

"Well, Janey," Dr. Campbell became the voice of the board, "would you let us professionals know what therapy you are using on Shelly and Johnson?"

"Aren't they any better?" she cried, alarmed.

"As far as we can tell, they are. They're both taking an interest in living. They're coming to the dining room together and eating well. And the last two evenings they've come to the game room to learn how to play pinochle."

"Oh, dear," said Janey, who had never learned. Pinochle was Jimmy's favorite card game.

"Well, Janey?" asked Dr. Kathryn.

"Mrs. Johnson is trying to stop being a raddled old stump, and Miss Shelly is practising freedom."

"Break it down," ordered Campbell.

"It's very simple. They're both feeling sorry for the other one, so they're helping each other."

"Helping each other," came in muted tones from all around the table.

"Looking out instead of in," stated Dr. Campbell.

They said to run along and keep on being herself, and Janey ran along. In fact, she flew. She'd caught one horrible glimpse of Grandma, her north end where her south end should have been; head down in the tiny creek that edged the far side of the tanbark.

By the time Janey reached her she'd levered herself up by her elbows. She couldn't use her hands; they were filled with bunches of wild ox-tails, fern fronds and of all things, twigs.

"Quarter cup of oatmeal. Oh, and my glasses fell off in the creek. Would you mind?"

This, thought Janey frantically, was all she needed: Grandma with her mind fractured. She found the glasses. The quarter cup of oatmeal she refused to search for.

"Janey, the oatmeal," Grandma reminded her as they headed toward the X Cabin, away from the dining hall. "Oh, silly, I want you to ask the cook for some. I need snow."

"Snow?" ventured Janey cautiously.

"One of the maids brought me a twig picture. Janey, you should have seen it. It was utterly impossible, so I thought I would show what could be done. I'm starting with a snow scene."

Janey listened, slightly bewildered, until she heard her grandmother ask if it would be all right to turn the arm of Cabin X, from which the bunks had been removed, into a studio. She spoke of field trips to choose species for drying, and of asking Jimmy if he'd mind taking her shopping at Gresham. She wasn't quite up to taking the bus yet.

Dutifully Janey turned back to the kitchen to hear "Sunflower seeds if you can buy them; I don't mind the salt. Janey, stop looking that way; they make excellent footprints in the snow."

Janey swung by the board room to ask permission to use the cabin arm. "Fine," said Campbell. "I'll send a carpenter over to put in bins." Janey wandered on to the kitchen. This was catching. Bins to her were mammoth scoops for flour and sugar. There were also small ones to hold seeds, and Grandma's hobby had once been seed pictures.

Lucky we're not in Cabin 7, she thought, and remembered what Sally had said.

A glance at her watch and she hurried to the administration building. It was time for Meg's hobby break. Meg was working in wool; this was something she could handle on the job during her spare time. Besides, she'd never been really warm in her life. She'd have afghans and sweaters and socks and caps.

"Hm," buzzed Janey, sinking into a chair.

Two-ton Tony and the angry man walked by, heading for a trail. How different they looked. Both had slowed down, but both were walking with an easy, swinging stride.

Sharon came in to check on the cost of a long distance call she'd made and didn't want on her bill.

Janey thought her boss would be happy to pay for it but didn't say so; instead she remarked how gay Sharon looked.

"It's working," Sharon reported solemnly. "I felt better even on the second day. Now, two weeks later, I rarely have those spells. Janey, will they go away altogether? You can't imagine the dreadful feeling."

Janey was sure they would, and when Sharon grew pensive and unhappy and confessed she might die of a virus because she'd be afraid of treatment, Janey automatically intoned, "When you know it doesn't make any difference whether you do or you don't, you won't. I mean worry, because you'll know what to do."

Sharon left, peace and assurance restored.

Queer how that rule helped everyone but herself. Her heart always turned a breath-taking flip flop when Jimmy came in. And she braced to defend herself.

Jimmy came in, and Janey's heart remained where it belonged. Nor did she brace herself. Jimmy was losing weight. And he had circles under his eyes that even the horn-rimmed glasses couldn't disguise.

"What a relief to find you alone," he greeted her, came in, sat down and put his feet up. "I'm bushed."

Janey's lips parted; then she brought them together. She would pretend Jimmy was a guest at the farm. Now what would she say to a guest?

"You're looking better," he offered. "Not that you're gaining any weight, but your color's good, and there's something in your eyes. Don't get it."

"It's not worrying about whether you do or you don't because then you won't."

162

Back came that look, and down went his feet.

But Janey was seeing Jimmy as a guest. "Like finding out you don't have to do a lifetime's work in a year. When you find it won't make any difference in the long run, you don't knock yourself out."

"But it does make a difference," he snapped. "I have to earn money fast. That means hopping onto every shadow of a new account."

"Are you in debt?"

"You know I'm not."

Ah, then, it was Stella. He thought he'd have to give her the life to which she'd been accustomed. Now how, with her own heart beginning to ache, could she save Jimmy's health with a theory that wasn't working too well for herself?

She would think of him as a guest and nothing more.

"Isn't Stella improving wonderfully?" she began, stammering a little. "She's a good example of the fact that material riches don't bring happiness. Do you know, Jimmy, she's even learning to cook?"

"She'd better," he replied morosely.

"And she's joined a sewing class. The best part of it is, she's having fun. She's also learning the value of money."

"Ha," said Jimmy.

Well, she could try further. She told how Stella

163

kept sending to her home for clothes, for books, for knickknacks to fix up her cabin.

"She didn't want anything from there, but when she found out how little money she had, she began being practical. She has lots of things to furnish a home, and she won't need clothes for years, she says."

"Lucky for both. Oh, doggone, here comes your watchdog. Janey, if I didn't owe that guy a lot for swinging this account to me, I'd wring his neck."

Janey had a tender picture of tall, gangling Jimmy making any impression on that bronze neck rising from a sports shirt to support the handsomest head north of Hollywood.

"Hello, Rainey; bring the proofs out with you? Oh? Well, if it's Miss Shelly—"

Jim arose to his full height. Janey, knowing him, watched words forming, rising, and shrank back, awaiting a blast that could ruin him with the health and beauty farm.

Instead he sneezed, a great wracking sneeze that shook his entire frame.

"Better come over to the infirmary with me," Nick said paternally. "You don't look up to par."

"Just a little summer cold. Well, got to get on with it; running up to Timberline." He hesitated a moment, looking at Janey, and Janey wondered if she'd be fool enought to trot at his heels if he suggested she join him.

Nick saved her from making a decision. He

164

handed her a card. "We'd like you to double-check this one. Dr. Kathryn settled her in, but—"

And he said, "Ah, not with that cold," as Jimmy would have kissed her cheek.

Janey walked out to the car with Jimmy and so did Nick. So she left them alone together and trotted off, for once curiosity overcoming concern about Jimmy.

The card read: "Phony."

One of the lesser cabins, Janey noted, and planned her approach. It wasn't necessary.

"My word, what are you doing here?" demanded the young woman repairing makeup before a mirror. "You're a knockout without farming."

"Cultivating," corrected Janey absently. "I came to lose weight."

"You sure made it. Then you stayed on to keep down?"

"Not exactly. I remained because there was work here I liked. One thing I do is take guests over the trails. Would you like to go for a walk?"

"Are you kidding? No, you're not. I thought only old folks who didn't have any place to go went for walks. Other guests go along?"

"Never more than two at a time; otherwise it becomes a gab fest."

The woman, listed as Mary Jones, told Janey to sit down and, once she was down, began asking questions and apologizing for asking. "I've just

165

got to know about everything and everybody. Born that way. You don't mind?"

Janey didn't mind. Neither did she answer.

"Say, you don't give out much," Miss Jones commented eventually.

"Would you like me to go to these women you've been asking about and tell them you wanted to know what they did, what visitors they had from outside, whom they were seeing, if they did much telephoning outside and how often they left the farm and with whom?"

Alarm sprang into the sharp blue eyes; then there came a shrug of the shoulders. "Wouldn't make for friendly living would it?" she asked. "I thought that was what this place advertised."

"That's why we don't answer personal questions." Janey smiled. "I see you like mysteries; you'll find some fine new ones in the library."

Aware she was being watched, Janey took her time returning. She found that easy. Every guest who passed stopped to talk, or Janey turned and walked with them a few feet. Eventually she returned to the administration building.

"She's interested in Carol or Sharon or Stella, I couldn't tell which. She knew an amazing lot about all three of them. She's not a professional investigator because she's too obvious. I'd say someone hired her to gather general information. Why is she supposed to be here?"

"Incipient melancholia following divorce and

recent major surgery," Nick read from the file code.

"Where is she from?"

"Manzanita."

"Dr. Kathryn would have a right to communicate with her doctor, wouldn't she? And if he were attending any of the others—but wait. Let me try out the name of the home town on the three."

Carol knew of the town but doubted she had more than driven through. Sharon didn't recognize it.

"Manzanita?" asked Stella. "We have a beach home just beyond there. Mother would know. She spends a lot of time garden-clubbing, that sort of thing, to say nothing of do-gooding."

Soberly Janey told the board members at dinner, "I have a feeling Mama has planted a gal in our midst to watch daughter."

"She's getting ready to pounce," Dr. Campbell agreed, "but we can't tell Stella yet; she's not ready. She'd panic. Janey?"

Janey drew a breath from her heart. If Mama pounced she'd have Jimmy back. But did she want him on the rebound?

Chapter Fourteen

Dr. Kathryn said she would get in touch with Miss Shelly's doctor. He would be able to confirm their suspicions. If the suspicions proved valid, they would decide what to do to protect Miss Shelly.

"Send this Jones woman packing," said Nick.

"But we will have identified her," Janey protested. "The next one Mama sent might be clever. What's more, I'd be suspicious of any new person coming in, and how could I be myself?"

They all laughed and all agreed, then worried about Miss Jones following Carol Johnson's car when she took Stella wherever the two of them chose to go on their many trips.

"Why not tell Mrs. Johnson?" suggested Janey. "Stella's been so good for her. She might take a real interest in protecting her. And she could alert us when they were going out and let us plan a delaying action on the Jones person."

"Good. You ask Mrs. Johnson if she'll see me within the hour."

Janey sped on her mission. But when she told Carol Dr. Kathryn wanted to see her, the crooked smile appeared on Carol's lips.

"Is the raddled old stump spoiling the farm garden?" she asked.

"Oh, dear me, no," cried Janey, "it isn't you she wants to see—I mean talk to. Oh, dear, I mean I'm not supposed to tell you, but I'd better. It's about Stella. You've done her so much good, they think, if you will, you should be the one to protect her. They know it's an awful lot to ask, but they have to have someone trustworthy."

"Mama?" asked Carol, and now her whole face was alive.

"They think so, and can't take a chance until Stella has her own feet, not Mama's, under her."

There was no question now of Carol's response. Eyes that had been dull began to shine; slump shoulders straightened. Her own life might be in a shambles, but she'd see that Stella was given a chance.

"Do you know," she confided, slipping into a becoming sweater, in lieu of one quite drab, "Stella even has me interested in the wilds. She brought tons of books on wildflowers and birds and even stars so she'd know how to find her way back if she were ever lost."

Janey rushed out with tears in her eyes. Jimmy had taught her all of those things. Stella must be trying to make ready for intelligent conversation with him when they settled in the weekend cabin.

She wondered if they'd bought it yet.

"What did you say?" asked Grandma McBride.

Janey had said that maybe in time, if she could find someone more whipped than she was, she might forget Jimmy and find another man. She doubted it.

"I said," she began bravely, "every woman should have an absorbing hobby. Why can't I find one?"

"I think you have." Grandma had brought her work to the circle room and was painstakingly picking up sunflower seeds with tweezers and carefully placing them on the oatmeal snow.

"Why, Gram, that's good; it's even beautiful. The way you prop the oatmeal on that twig makes it look like a real tree, snow-burdened. I could never do that."

"Good idea if you could; it would take your mind off Jimmy. I didn't mean this." The last pseudo footprint in place, she straightened. "I meant your flair for helping people. Nick was raving about you. I think the man thinks he's in love with you."

"Thinks he is!" bridled Janey.

"He's emotionally cautious. He'd never let himself go until he was sure you were cured of Jimmy. He'll probably find a way to do that. He's succeeded in all of the preliminary steps thus far."

"Grandma! With my own ears I heard Stella ask about Jimmy the moment she saw him. I introduced them. They didn't need any help from Nick."

"I wasn't speaking of that; I was referring to his adroit way of getting you out here so he could carry on his campaign without having to drive to the city. You're really a very beautiful girl, Janey, and an asset to the farm."

"If you mean he'd marry me to keep me here you're dreaming. And who says I'm beautiful?"

"Your mirror, if you ever give it a chance."

Janey went to the full length mirror and Mrs. McBride's voice followed. "You've been so concerned with your shape you've never taken a full view of yourself. Try looking at your face for a change."

Janey looked at her face. She wanted to wail. How could anyone with a broken heart look so healthy, with an apple blossom complexion, hair now its own natural pale gold, and those eyes?

"My eyes always seemed to have been put in by mistake," she murmured. "My kind of face should have blue ones and blond lashes. Instead the brows and lashes look inked in, false."

With a look of defeat, her grandmother rose and came to her. "Janey, Dr. Campbell told me I should reveal something to you. It doesn't seem right, but it's better than hearing you disparage yourself.

"You were such a beautiful child Grandpa feared you'd grow up vain. So he picked imaginary flaws. He overdid it. I tried to make up by buying you the prettiest clothes I could find; then he put a stop to that. He was a fine man, but prejudiced about beauty in women. You see, a great beauty turned him down before he married me. It took him forty years to get over her."

"But he did?"

"He did. She'd depended entirely on physical beauty, and when it faded she had nothing left. That made him more than ever determined to keep you from realizing your blessing.

"Then Jimmy came along and put the finishing touches on Grandpa's work. The two men who meant the most to you refused to see you were beautiful. And you are."

Janey tiptoed out of the X Cabin. She tiptoed on up the path to the dining hall. She was a little late. Bemused, she made an entrance, and everyone in the place looked up; every man on the board leaped to draw out a chair for Janey.

"Child, what have you done to yourself?" asked Dr. Kathryn.

"Grandma just told me something," breathed Janey.

"Hm," buzzed Dr. Campbell, looked over at Nick and said, "Now *she* knows it." Nick frowned.

If only Jimmy would drive in, thought Janey. Now that she knew, she could act beautiful before him, and maybe he'd see that even though she wasn't plump she was lovely to look at.

But Jimmy didn't drive in that evening or on any other. Janey hovered around Stella, hoping to

172

heard some word of him. If Stella knew anything, she wasn't broadcasting with Janey around.

If only she hadn't become unengaged to him she could have telephoned to invite him out. Why hadn't she waited? With this new, priceless knowledge she might have won out over Stella, who really wasn't even pretty.

No wonder she had chosen modeling; Grandma had explained about the dowdy clothes of her girlhood. She'd had "a deficiency," said Janey.

Jimmy wasn't telephoning or driving or even working. Jimmy was reposing in Room 404 of Good Samaritan Hospital. He'd sneezed once too often, right in front of Enid Stedman who, with Janey's interests at heart, had ordered her husband to order him into the hospital.

Husband and wife talked it over in their split level house overlooking the river.

"I just don't understand it," said Mrs. Stedman. "Janey hasn't called the office once, has she?"

"Probably doesn't know he's sick. Now wait; don't you go mixing in this. They've had some kind of a misunderstanding."

"It's that Nick Larson," declared Mrs. Stedman. "It must be. No girl could live around him without falling half in love with him."

"Don't be too sure. When Jim was delirious he kept talking about Stella. I think he meant the Shelly girl. She's out at the farm now. Guess you

173

heard what happened to her, even if it wasn't in the papers."

"Why, that lovely Janey child is worth a dozen Shilly-Shally Shellys with the Shelly millions thrown in."

"I wouldn't mind picking up a few of the Shelly accounts," came the wistful rejoinder.

"Joseph Charles Stedman, if you are egging that boy on to win an account through—"

"I only suggested it and my employee had the temerity to pin my ears back. He said if he accomplished anything with the Shellys, it would be to separate that poor girl from the whole kit and caboodle of them. I didn't repeat the suggestion."

Joe spent a bad night. His wife was ill. She said he'd have to call his sister and let her take their children for a return call.

By dawn he agreed to spare her a few weeks if she could get a reservation at the beauty farm after he'd reserved a convalescent cottage for Jimmy. He was to pay for both.

He'd argued, but he'd had a hard day. Jimmy left a big gap in the office.

Meg took the reservations, then relayed the call on to the board room. Only Dr. Campbell was in.

"Hm," said Dr. Campbell.

Lola came home unexpectedly. She found Janey looking more beautiful than ever, looking positively radiant in Nick's arms. The arms were both wound around so Janey had to tip back her head and look up adoringly.

Meg, who had thrown away her pad, used scratch paper as she tried to bring the women's physical director up to date.

"But Janey's not engaged to Jimmy any more," Meg tried to defend her friend when Lola expressed her opinion of engaged girls who made public spectacles of themselves.

"Why isn't she?" demanded Lola.

Meg answered easily, "Because Jimmy likes his girls well padded, and Janey doesn't gain now, no matter what she eats. She stays perfect."

Lola waited only a moment. Then she wheeled, said she'd be back in a couple of days, warned Meg to say nothing of her visit, and took off. Actually, she thumbed a ride to the city.

There she managed to hail a taxi, thumb still up. She came to at the airport, trying to thumb a ride on a south-bound plane before she realized she, the poised, the ever rational, had flipped.

Janey, floating into the office to relieve Meg, was told Lola had come in for her mail, then taken off again.

"Boy, was she ever upset at finding you nuzzling your chin on Nicky's shoulder!" Meg commented.

"He is the dearest, most thoughtful man I ever met," mused Janey. "He had his arms all ready when he told me about Jimmy being desperately ill."

Meg, who'd caught a glimpse of Janey's face, shook her head. Just why should that make Janey so happy?

"Love," stated Meg.

"It's so wonderful when you've reached the state of not caring whether you do or you don't,'' agreed Janey, and flew away.

It was wonderful, she thought, and stretched up her arms to all the beauty around her. Jimmy was coming to spend a month at the farm. Janey didn't care if he spent hours with Stella; just knowing he was out of danger was enough for her.

But she'd better go into conference with Carol Let word get back to Mama that Stella was seeing too much of a man with few prospects of wealth, social position or fame, and Mama would break the sound barrier with a blast that would destroy Stella.

Dr. Campbell was way ahead of her. Even with new cabins going up as fast as overtime workmen could erect them, reservations were coming in faster than guests could be accommodated.

"This Miss Jones," he told the board members, "is a fly in our general ointment. She irritates guests. I also believe, having found nothing to report, she is sending out false statements. Dr. Kathryn, you could conscientiously report her cured?"

Dr. Kathryn nodded, recalling her findings. "Her divorce was three years ago, her surgery two. Physically she is perfect. As she refuses psychotherapy, we have every right to discharge her."

And Mary Jones, who'd thought she had weeks ahead of a life of ease, went out with fury in her eyes and acid on her tongue.

The Joe Stedmans, James Rainey and Lola converged upon the farm on the same day.

Fortunately Janey wasn't there to see Jimmy literally lifted out of the station wagon and carried to a cabin on the upper level, away from the farm proper. Joe Stedman and one Ward Dyck, a male attendant, did the carrying.

That was the day Carol Johnson had to go to the city on estate matters. Stella still refused to risk crossing even the city limits. Maybe she was twenty-five, but she remembered a few days of rebellion at seventeen when she'd been whisked out of a parked car by her mother's minions.

Stella had bought a car of sorts with some jewelry; gifts from her brothers. Carol had taught her to drive. Janey, ready to give her all for the wonderful health and beauty farm, risked life and limb to accompany Stella on a trip that day.

"Isn't this a sweetheart?" Stella asked, patting the car's fenders as they embarked. "It's the first thing I ever owned completely. Why, do you know every time I'd had a doll long enough to love it,

Mama would take it away, saying, 'Oh, stop playing with that dirty old thing; here's a new one.' "

Stella took a devious way of going some place. Janey was rapidly lost until Stella said brightly, "This is Eagle Creek, a wonderful trout stream."

Finally she drove down a woods-rutted road and pulled up before a building.

"Isn't it beautiful?" she demanded of Janey.

Janey swallowed twice before she remembered a phrase from school days. If beauty lay in the eye of the beholder, Stella needed corrective glasses.

"It's mine," Stella explained, "and only you and Carol know where it's located."

"Not even Jimmy?"

"Oh, he'll see it some day. Come on."

Obediently Janey followed her up a painfully cleared path and waited as she unlocked padlocks and patent locks, went inside and unlocked windows.

Janey caught her breath as she entered. Now this was beautiful in a woodsy way. Windows opened onto the forest; one large window, newly installed, looked up Eagle Creek to a vista of mountains.

A new fireplace was flanked by shelves filled with books. A kitchen was stocked with canned goods, and Janey smiled, remembering a patent can opener.

"I made the curtains and drapes," Stella said proudly, "and the cushions. Meg's going to teach me to knit, and I'll make afghans. But just think, Janey, it's mine."

When they left, Stella locked the door and stood looking at the cabin. "Isn't it wonderful how shabby it looks on the outside? That's why I had shutters put on the windows. I've learned a valuable lesson. If from the outside nothing shows its value, nobody will try to take it from me.

"You know," she put the car in gear, "it's like marrying a Greek god. All the women would be forever fighting to take him away. Choose someone fine but not handsome."

"Like Jimmy," breathed Janey, going down in final defeat.

"Umhum, like Jimmy."

They reached the farm, and Janey escaped to the X Cabin to find it empty. That was unusual. Grandma attracted people as honey attracted flies, and since her snow scene had been put on display in the lounge she had a growing class of "twig and seed" artists.

With tremendous self-sacrifice Janey cut down the time she saw Jimmy to one minute out of every sixty minutes, or twelve minutes a day, more or less. Even though she now knew she was beautiful, much more beautiful than Stella, she couldn't use that beauty to destroy Stella.

Hadn't Stella warned her against marrying a man like dear, precious Nick Larson? Look how Lola suffered every time a woman looked at him, and Lola was beautiful. So beauty alone couldn't hold a man.

And didn't Lola know it? She had Dr. Campbell by the lapel, literally backed into a corner, a sheaf of notes in one hand waving in front of his nose.

"I demand you do something!" she said, black eyes flashing.

"Hm," said Dr. Campbell.

Chapter Fifteen

"If you say hm again I'll scream," warned Lola.

"Now, Lola, remember you're a staff member, not a guest. No time for aberrations; we've overloaded with people who need our service. But interesting, most interesting. Valuable bit of research you did here, regardless of your motives."

"If you'd seen Janey as I did—" Lola's voice was tight. "Maybe you don't know and others don't know and she doesn't know she's in love with Nick, but I do! And you've got to do something, fast."

"Yes, of course. Staff relationships must be kept harmonious regardless of whose heart is broken, eh? You're just trying to make sure it isn't yours. You should try Janey's panacea."

"Bah," said Lola, and stalked off.

Grandma McBride was making a leisurely way to the X Cabin. Like any mother, she'd seen her chick come in with her feathers ruffled and had bided her time.

"Well, Janey, I thought you'd be up welcoming Jimmy to the farm."

"He's here? Oh, w y hold a burned arm to the fire?"

"In my childhood that's how people drew out inflammation, or thought they did. I wonder what they did do." But she was talking to thin air.

As Janey explained to herself, she should think of Jimmy's point of view. She must make him feel at ease, no matter what it cost her.

It cost quite a bit. Jimmy without his glasses looked so defenseless. Where he'd been thin before, he was now emaciated, and so pale one couldn't tell where his face left off and the pillow began.

"Oh, Jimmy, I'm so glad you're here where we can take care of you."

"Planned it that way," he boasted. "You're to sunsit me while Ward takes time off."

"Ward? Oh, Ward Dyke, the man who's—" Her voice trailed away. This Ward Dyke certainly didn't look like a male nurse. He was bronzed, husky, and so easy going Janey felt alarms and nerves and fears disappear.

The next three weeks were the most wonderful Janey had ever lived. She didn't know it, but she grew more beautiful by the hour; the hour she spent on the terrace timing the amount of sun Jimmy should have on that particular day.

Mrs. Stedman ran some kind of interference. She sidetracked visitors so Jimmy wouldn't have too many callers.

Later, when Jimmy began taking walks, Mrs. Stedman maneuvered things so Stella went with Ward while either she or Janey, if she were free, walked with Jimmy.

Sometimes Dr. Campbell took him off alone.

Jimmy grew tanned and slowly began putting on weight.

Janey went to the dietitian. "Please tell me what you're feeding him so I can gain too."

"Same as you. Mr. Rainey had a food compulsion. He ingested such vast quantities of unrelated food nothing was digested. He devoured at the same time food that required acid and food that required alkaline properties to effect digestion. They cancelled each other out."

Defeated, Janey gave up. She was just stuck with her figure, which everyone but Jimmy thought perfect.

The health and beauty farm boomed as summer strode in with blazing sun and blazing flower gardens. The woods offered such delicious shade, walks were no problem.

Guests came in frowning and went out smiling to make room for more frowners and to spread the astonishing effect this simple farm had had upon their lives.

And Janey went spinning around like a top, being herself.

Grandma went to the city to shop and returned with boxes marked Elaine's and the little dresser, whom she'd invited to use the upper bunk in the one room now containing bunks at the X Cabin. Meg had taken over an arm for the wool class.

"Gram, don't you need some money?" whispered Janey when the dresser was settled.

"Dear child, didn't I tell you? I'm making so much teaching my hobby the farm has decided to hire me on salary on a year-round basis. I'll have a cabin of my own after the heavy season's over."

Janey felt so giddy at this news, she didn't pay too much attention to what the dresser said on their walk.

"And Limey heard every word. This Nick wanted you fired so he could have you at the farm. He said it was for your good, psychologically speaking. But first he wanted you to have time to prove you couldn't stay toothpick thin.

"Leave it to Elaine to go him one better; she fixed up that salmon lamé. Then that girl, Lola something, jumped the gun and played right into their hands."

"Oh," said Janey, and sat down on a stump. Grandma had been right. Nick might be as handsome as a Greek god, but he was a calculator, a manipulator, and she'd die before she'd marry a man like that.

She felt bereft. Not until she heard this did she realize how she'd counted on having Nick as a last resort, a balm to her pride.

When they returned to the farm proper, she forgot all about it. The place milled; people, even cabins, seemed going around in circles. The center of the vortex was a superlative car with a stiff-necked chauffeur standing guard.

"Oh, my goodness," cried Janey, "it's Mama," and flew to the rescue of Stella.

But Stella wasn't present. Stella's cabin held no signs of occupancy. Carol Johnson was also missing.

Nick caught up with her. "Janey, where is she?"

Mama Shelly, thundering down in his wake, demanded. "Produce her or I'll wipe this place from existence."

"Why did you come visiting today?" Janey flashed.

"I was told of the goings-on here. I was informed there was a plot to kidnap my child. Now, young woman, who took her away from here and where was she taken?"

A carload of reporters and cameramen came in on two wheels, and for the first time Janey saw Nick blanch. "Think of the publicity, Janey," ordered Nick. "It was bad enough when you were lost."

"I was not lost," she protested. Neither was Stella, she thought. Stella had probably received word of Mama's invasion and moved to her cabin. Janey had promised she wouldn't reveal its location.

185

"Hey, Miz Shelly, ransom note come in yet?" one of the more brazen reporters called.

Janey could imagine the headlines: "Shelly heiress kidnapped from beauty farm."

Where did her loyalty lie?

Nick saw Dr. Campbell coming and steered Mama that way, and Janey ducked under arms to meet the press.

"You boys are going to look awfully silly when the truth comes out," she said, and flew for the woods circling around to Jimmy's cabin.

"Jimmy," she whispered, "come out from wherever you are."

He came out, blinking.

"Do you know how to reach Stella's cabin? Has she ever told you?"

"Got a map somewhere. Why? Hey, what's all the fuss down there?"

"Stella's been kidnapped and Mama's blaming the farm."

"Kidnapped? She has not. She's out getting married and doesn't want to be interrupted."

"Married?" asked Janey, eyes like an owl's. How could she? Or was she being married by proxy?

"To Edward. You know, the guy who's been giving me a hand. We thought this a good way to bring them together again. You've heard me speak of Ed; one good guy. You know, he was the fellow

186

she was engaged to first. And Mama broke up the deal."

Janey thought of her weeks of torture. "James Rainey, why did you let me believe you were going to marry her?"

"I never did. I've been trying to help these two, and believe me, it took doing. I'd take Stella to dinner where Ed would just happen to be, and take her driving and just happen to see Ed, and finally they came to.

"Stella hadn't gone through with her other engagements because it was Ed she loved all the time. That's why she decided to duck out on life. Mama wouldn't let her have Ed, or anything else she wanted, so why live?"

"And Edward became Ward because Ed or Edward would have alerted mama. Oh, dear, who's going to break the news to Mama?"

"It will be a pleasure." Jimmy adjusted his glasses and his shoulders, threw back a: "Sit down; I want to talk to you," and strode off.

After fifteen minutes he strode back.

"Now why would I want to marry Stella?" he asked.

"Because you thought her beautiful."

"She is in a way, but a little on the fat side. You, Janey, you're really beautiful."

But Janey was wary. "You mean I'm not too thin?"

"Campbell gave me a run-down on that. He had

187

to. I was in a bad way, Janey. I loved you and I hated you at the same time. That's why I treated you so rotten. When I found out why I hated you, I found out I didn't."

Janey supposed that made sense, but she needed to know more. If he should ever hate her again, she wanted to know what to do about it.

"Doc did some research on my background," Jimmy continued. "He found out my mother had been a lovely woman. She died when I was two, and I didn't remember anything but the security I had had in her arms. My aunt took me over.

"She's a good woman, never overlook that, but she had funny ideas about food. And she was thin as a rail; still is. I half starved all during my growing years, for food and for affection, and somehow I associated slenderness with a form of extreme attrition. To me, someone real plump was the antithesis."

That made sense, but surely there was something more. Janey heard voices; people were coming their way.

"Come on." Jimmy grabbed her by the arm, and they shot into the woods to walk quite a distance before they stopped on a wooded knoll that gave a view of Mt. Hood.

Jimmy took up the tale, once he was assured they would be left alone.

"So then Doc went on with his explanation. I was cracking up because I really loved you, re-

188

gardless of whether you looked like a barrel or a slat. This 'Love is blind' is the real McCoy. You don't love a person because of his beauty or lack of it; it's something deeper. So now will you marry me right away? Or do you love that Greek god?"

"He can't marry until the season's over," Janey mused. "And I'm afraid he wouldn't be marrying me; he'd be marrying an asset to the farm. I'd hate to be loved for that, wouldn't you?"

Mt. Hood looked down. A cloud of snow blew over his face.

"This sickness has set me back a bit," Jimmy confided, "but I'm doing all right. How about that split-level, with a view of mountain and river?"

"Now that Grandma is happily self-supporting, why don't we settle for an apartment?" And Janey mentally added: There will be no room for visiting friends and relations and no furnace room. She loved the farm, but she didn't want to return as a guest.

If your dealer does not have any of the MAGNUM EASY
EYE CLASSICS, send price of book plus 10 cents to cover
postage to MAGNUM CLASSICS, 18 East 41st Street, Room
1501, New York, N.Y. 10017.